WITCH

WITCH

FINBAR HAWKINS

ZEPHYR

An imprint of Head of Zeus

First published in the UK in 2020 by Zephyr,
an imprint of Head of Zeus Ltd
This paperback edition first published in 2021 by Zephyr,
an imprint of Head of Zeus Ltd

9 7 5 3 1 2 4 6 8

A catalogue record for this book is available from
the British Library.

ISBN (PB): 9781838935627
ISBN (E): 9781838935634

Typeset and designed by Ed Pickford and Luna Ait-Oumeghar

Printed and bound in Great Britain by
CPI Group (UK) Ltd, Croydon CRO4YY

Head of Zeus Ltd
First Floor East
5–8 Hardwick Street
London ECIR 4RG

WWW.HEADOFZEUS.COM

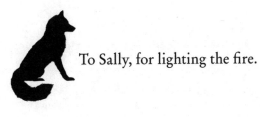 To Sally, for lighting the fire.

'...Oh witchinge eies, and wit, where wit and
    eies maie Reade,
A witche, and not a witche, and yet a witche
    indeede.'

Nicholas Breton, *My Witche* (1617)

'*Thou shalt not suffer a witch to live.*'

Exodus 22:18
King James Bible (1611)

Where my Dilly Dee, my Dilly Dear,
will you go, my Dilly Doe?
Tell Mother where you are,
my sweet dancer of the day.

Why, I chase the rabbits, Mother,
the day that will be,
the wind that blows,
the sun that smiles like me.

Then go, Dilly Dee, Dilly Doe,
chase them as you may,
my Dilly dear,
my dancer of the day.

I never did no magick.

Not at the time they said, anyways.

It was Mother who heard them. Mother could hear a frog hiccup from a mile yonder. She could whisper out a blackcap nesting in the trees. Mother had old ways, from far across the sea. And that's what she looked to teach us. Perhaps that's what led to it all. All the blood. And the death.

When Mother hollered us, I didn't see them. Dill pointed down.

'There, Eveline, there low!'

I saw them. The skulkers. Men. Horses. They were coming. They knew us.

No matter that Mother healed them. Cured their stock. Smacked their children into the world. Here they came, like whelps. Boys to fetch us in. Scared. Angry. Men.

'Dill, get!'

We ran fleet foot, wind after catching us, and we found Mother, leaning on her staff. She pressed a bag to me. She was pale as birch bark. She could not run. Her leg was twisted and scarred like a root grown wrong.

'They're coming!' Dill pulled at Mother, who only bent to stroke dirt from her cheek.

'Here, my Dilly Dee...'

She opened Dill's hand to place something. It sat round and black and heavy on Dill's thin fingers. The Wolf Tree Stone. Mother's scrying stone. Then she looked me sharp.

'Get to the coven. Find my sister. Look to Dill. Go now!'

I remember that. Her face like wax settled on wood. Her lips split. Her eyes all fire.

'Evey, swear you will ever look to Dill.'

Her face so fierce with love. I heard shouts. They were close.

'For my blood, your blood, your sister's blood...' She pushed against me. 'Swear it and go, Evey!'

And this I have of her always. Her mouth, shouting, furious at me.

'I do swear it, Mother...' Then I took Dill's hand and we ran.

We ran to the near wood. Like rabbits before the dogs. That's what they were, see. Not men, but dogs that stank and slavered. We made the trees when I heard a shriek that shanked deep as a knife.

Dill wanted back, but that wouldn't be. She pulled at me, kicked and scratched. Mother let shriek again. I remember her cry, like a fox snared.

'Evey, they're hurting her… EVEY!'

But I held Dill fast. She gripped Mother's stone, her fingers tight white.

'Hush it, Dill – we'll be caught.'

There were four of them. They had broken her staff. They had ripped her dress. Mother brought her arm to her breasts, as she swayed upon her good leg, her dark hair flying, her eyes coals in the fire.

I knew then. She saw her end.

And in that moment, she saw theirs.

'Touch not my children!' Her voice echoed to the watching sky. 'Or I swear it, you all…' She pointed at the four who watched her. 'You all will die!'

She was so strong, so beautiful, so alone.

Then one came close and struck her face.

I felt it like he struck my own. I stopped my mouth from crying out.

Mother fell.

How I wanted to run to her. Swing high to skewer those dogs. But I had no blade. They were too many. And I would break Mother's bond.

Go, Evey. For me. For Dill.

My sister twisted like a wild cat. But I held her good, as a tall one turned about, as if he caught our scent. Quick I pulled Dill lower as she moaned over.

'Mother, Mother, Mother...' Her fingers pulling at mine.

And my guts churned with shame for our hiding, as I marked him, this Tall One with his long black hat. He raised his arm high, like as to hail me. Then let it fall, and his men sprang to. Laughing, shouting, they lifted Mother, as she struggled in their grip.

I couldn't go. They were too many.

Evey.

They brought Mother to the ground and laid her arm. And the largest, he ran and he jumped, like a boy at play. He jumped and snapped her arm. That sound, breaking like an old branch in the wood where we hid. He snapped her arm. And Mother shrieked and rolled as they laughed like dogs. Like men.

They closed around her. I could not see.

Please.

Four men.

For me.

They beat her.

For Dill.

Over and again.

Go. Now.

Then I felt it.

I could not run to her, but I could curse them.

So I did. I cursed them with all my fury.

'Know this, I will not rest till balance got.
Till time turned back. Till light be sought.
Till dogs be dirt and death be done.
Till then. Only then, know this.'

I held Dill's face to my chest, away from their blows.

They shouted with glee. They pushed her down. Still she raised to her knees, her arm hanging as a spider's thread broken in the breeze.

'My children!'

Her voice echoed, so that I will ever hear it. There was stillness and there was Mother and the men and us watching and our hearts beating.

Then another stepped forward. He was young, not yet a man. He raised his musket high.

Mother looked up to this brave boy. She spat.

He swore and swung that musket so swift and smote her skull. She rolled, then did not move, in the mud.

And we knew Mother was dead.

'No. NO!'

Dill pushed at me, crying, but I grabbed her mouth. She was little then. She wasn't strong much. Fast like a cat, but light as a bird was Dill.

'Shush, or we'll be got!' Pain tore my voice. 'Shush, now, Dill, you… you hear!'

Dill's tears ran over my hand, her eyes screaming. Yet she nodded, as she shook.

They were standing about Mother. Voices low, butchers weighing a pig. Some pissed. Like dogs. Like dogs. Then Tall One pushed and shouted at that brave boy who killed our mother.

'The witch was for trial, boy! We still have not the children!'

I felt cold creep across my body, my hairs standing. They knew us, sought us. The brave lad shouted back, for he was not afeared.

'You saw – she cursed me! You have to kill 'em quick so it will not take!'

He spat upon Mother and kicked her withered leg. I fought to snatch Mother's stone from Dill and run to him and smash his face. But I could not, I could not.

'Find them!' Tall One turned to that thin man, that heavy brute, that brave lad, all those dogs who I marked true. 'Find them now!'

We had to fly, Mother.

I cursed them and cursed them good. Everything you gave me, I gave to them.

Tall One roused his pack towards the woods.

We flew for our hearts.

We flew for you.

We were running in the dark wood, Dill close to.

Little she was, but she could fly all the same. Time past I chased her tawny legs through summer's dusk. When we ran as sisters not as rabbits, feared for our skins.

We fell to a stream, cupped our faces, drinking deep. Then we stood in the running water. Far-off shouts now, not near. Those dogs were slow.

A sparrow flitted to a branch above, and cried, *This way, this way, this way.* Dill breathed hard as she listened. The stream pressed cold about our feet. We saw ourselves in the water. Dill, skin and bone, pale as morning milk, her hair black and thick as a rook's nest. And me taller, my cheeks, my arms all mottled over, like drops of brown rain, my hair long and red. The colour of anger, Mother used to say. And the song she sang for me, came babbling through that green water.

'Evey Red Braid,
watch thy mist.
Evey Red Locks,
drop thy fist.'

Dill smiled to the girls in the water. The younger waved to see her. But her sister frowned and said, 'Silly mite. This is not the time for playing. Come now.'

We brooked the stream, smooth stones under foot and held at roots to make the bank. I listened true. No dog came barking. Dill's hand was soft and small as a mouse in mine. We passed through the wood, and after a time, we saw it, sitting far away, smoke lifting, like hair in the wind.

'Why there, Evey?' She pointed to town with her fist curled about the black stone.

'Because that's where dogs will home to sleep.'

And I swear, Mother. I never will let them lie. Only in death.

Only then.

Rain was after soaking us. The sky was lead. We had to shelter.

'I's wet to bone, Evey.'

'So's I, Dill. Won't kill you none.'

She coughed. Little toad. Ever I must look to her, ever she must play. When we made the coven, then she would know better.

Croake Farm crouched on the hill. We watched it, as the rain combed our tired heads.

'Evey...'

'Shush it, Dill. Wait and listen, will you?' I pulled her hand for quiet.

She did then, with a sniff. And there, the farm windows gleamed like the yellow eyes of a cat in the night.

I listened. The rain fell. Dill's hand moved in mine. I must nest this mouse else the rain would take her. And that wouldn't be. I swore to Mother I would look to her. She was just a child. Where I was a child no more.

A shadow moved cross a window. Chance we had then, to find warm. I pulled Dill on, and she followed, humming spite the cold.

We ran through the mud and the dark. Light from a window fell to the cobbles, slimy under our toes. A tree creaked like it moaned to be let in. I hammered the door, its sound echoing about that muddy yard. The wood was wet on my palm.

No sound, only the rain, hissing.

I knew this farm. Had cured stock here with Mother last summer. There was no danger. Still I steeled and tighter drew Dill's hand. I went to knock again.

A bolt shot and the door cracked. A man's face, I knowed him and he knowed me. His eyes moved to the dark, then to me.

'What... What do you want?' He was after being fierce, but I smelled fear upon him.

'Shelter,' I said over the rain. 'We need shelter... James Croake.'

I had found his name, and the old face looked up, eyes blinking.

'I am Eveline. This is Dill.' Water clogged my tongue.

'Hello, James Croake,' Dill coughed.

'I know who you are.' His eyes darted from us to the pressing dark. 'I cannot...'

He made to close his door. My hand went to hold it.

'Please...' I trembled, but I had to be strong. Had to find a way.

Dill coughed again. Croake looked down at her.

'Where is... your mother?' He knew it as quick as he said it.

I stepped closer, felt the light and warmth upon my face.

'They came. They...' My throat jabbed, like I had swallowed a needle. 'She is gone...'

Dill's thumb stroked over my shaking fist.

The old man stared at me with eyes rheumy and blue. His tongue turned with his thoughts. If he let us in, I knew that we would talk on it.

Then silent, he stepped back to open the door wide. Dill darted through, quick as you like, a little mouse happy to be home, stretching her arms through the warmth.

'I thank you kindly, old man Jim.' Even a smile rising upon her tired face.

'Come, then, if you're coming.'

He waved a hand, gnarled as the tree creaking in his yard. I nodded for his relenting, and I stepped into Croake Farm.

3

S hadows leaped about the walls, as Croake closed the door behind us. We breathed the heat from the hearth in the corner, the smell of sheep, smoke and broth. I moved my palm to the hearth, feeling the ash hot between my fingers.

Dill jumped up and the stone in her hand tapped against the slate. Ever she was holding it, whispering to it.

Croake limped to the fire. His breath rattled as he filled a bowl from the pot. I watched his mouth twitch.

'Here…' His hand shook slight as he offered the food.

'Thank you, James Croake.'

Dill bent to her bowl, the steam rising through her wet hair.

Croake passed same to me. I tasted parsley, carrot and turnip as I drank, feeling the broth fill and flow about me. A chair creaked. I lowered that bowl, and the old man sat by the fire, watching the window, then watching us. At last he spoke, at last he came to it, as I knew he would.

'I'm… sorry for… Your mother helped us. Helped our families hereabouts…'

Anger rose in me, like the steam from Croake's pot.

'Yes, Mother helped you…' And his broth was sweet no more. 'But now she is dead. Because of her witching way. Is that what you mean?'

I cast my words like stones. It was that same witching way I had told her I wanted no more on. But now she was gone and nothing could I tell her.

Croake cast his eyes down, as might a scolded child.

'Tell me, old man, will your sorry bring my mother back? Will your sorry—'

'Evey, it is not his fault!'

Dill buried her head to her knees, Mother's stone clutched in her paw, as she rocked, like a hedgehog balled. She fought the same pain that coursed me.

'Please don't fight him,' she said softer. 'Can we not rest?'

I scowled to the old man who watched the shadows.

'It is nobody's fault, sister,' I said. 'But her own. For witches are wicked, evil things and must be hunted.' My words simmered in spite. 'Everyone knows that. Don't they?'

Dill only turned from me, too tired to fight.

I drank again, but the knot would not wash from my throat. Croake kicked a log to the hearth and we fell to silence as the fire spat.

Dill yawned beneath her buried head. I shivered though I grew warmer and looked about. Some tools stood in a corner. A hoe and a scythe arching over the window. A table, a pair of chairs. Another door ajar showed a bed. Some rags beneath the window. They moved then growled.

'Shush there, Dog,' Croake muttered.

And just as she seemed won over by sleep, up Dill sprang with a cry,

'Ah, pups! Evey, look, now!'

She kneeled where a young bitch lay. 'Three, four… five little ones! What is her name?'

Croake gave a shrug, 'Just Dog.'

The dog's thin tail drummed the floor as Dill stroked her.

'She must have a name. I shall name her…' Dill put her face to the bitch's brown nose. 'Berry, for her eyes are black and she is sweet!'

She clicked her tongue. And so coaxed, Berry moved her head to Dill's leg and they lay together with those pups, all curled into sleep.

'The child has a way with beasts…'

'Why, yes, Jim Croake.' I licked the edge of my words. 'My sister has gifts. All animals are drawn to her.' I shivered again with a cold that curdled in my gut. I was prodding her, but I could not help it. Dill opened one eye to me.

'It is not a gift, Evey. I only like animals. And they like me.'

She looked with love at the slumbering pups. How I wanted to pinch her, pull her hair.

'And they do not like me.' My jaw hurt with gritting my teeth.

Dill brought her arm under the dog's head, and the stone caught firelight. Why did she cling to it so? Would it bring Mother back? Would it kill those men who took her from us?

'Birds do, if you let them.' She yawned. 'But I think you do not try to, sister.'

Her head turned back to that bed of bodies. How simple for Dill. She had lost Mother. She had been hunted. She had run for her life. And she had named a dog. In a day her world had spun. And yet, Dilly Doe danced on. She had a way all right. Mother knew it. But did Mother ever tell me I was gifted? Not never.

'What… is in the child's hand?' Croake's chair creaked, as he leaned to look.

Before I could utter, Dill lifted her head, her smile so white and proud. 'It is Mother's scrying stone. It has powers. Mother gave it me to keep safe for—'

'Powers?' Croake's eyes flickered. 'Is it magick?'

Dill sat up to stroke the stone like a drowsy pup.

'It is, Jim Croake, but only to those who know.' Her smile grew bigger still. 'Some things, Mother taught me…'

'It should be mine,' I said. 'Since I am the eldest.' My words pinched her. I could not help it. 'Since Mother is dead.'

Dill's smile dropped. 'Evey, Mother only meant for me to keep it safe.'

'And does that make it yours, sister dear?'

Her face was still and sad. 'Evey, I did not say it was—'

'Now Mother is dead, it should be mine.'

'Stop saying that!' She stood, shaking. 'Stop saying Mother is dead!'

'But she is.'

'I know! I saw! And you stopped me!'

The shadows hummed with her shout.

Tears lined her cheeks. But I felt raw, and empty. I wanted everyone to leave me be. Mother was dead. For ever.

'I had to stop you, Dill, the men were—'

'I don't care about it now.'

She turned from me to stroke Berry. 'Leave me alone. I want to sleep.'

It was as if all her spirit had gone, snuffed by me. She curled about the dogs and closed her eyes, the stone glimmering in her grasp.

I watched her fall to sleep. I had hurt her, goaded her. I did not know why. But I knew I would do it again. I could not help it. It was Mother's fault.

You're my clever little witch, Dilly.

And what did she ever say to me?

Be strong, Evey. Look to your sister, Evey.

'She minds me of my little Alice,' said Croake, watching Dill's head rise on Berry's flank. 'My granddaughter.'

I had seen Alice only once before. I remembered a scurry of smiles and curls.

'I lost her,' he said low. 'In the war...'

'I did not know it.'

It was as though my voice was not part of me. As though it came from another Evey standing alone in the corner of that dusty kitchen.

He bit his lip as he looked into the flames. 'Your mother...'

I felt that cold slide again in my belly. 'My mother? Have it out, Jim Croake. You have ridden that chair this long to it.'

His stare became harder, and the fire jumped in those old eyes.

'Well, then… Your mother showed Alice and others some of her ways… that she… and what they learned… It brought trouble. It must have…'

So finally, Croake had grasped to it, like a blind beggar to his stick.

I felt a shout rise in my chest. I wanted to push over his table, break his chair, kick out his hearth. So angry I was for it all. For Mother. Against my sister. Now at this old man's stupid stumble.

'Does it seem as right,' I swallowed the tears that welled within me, 'that a woman… who taught girls how elderflower might cure a fever. Who…'

I thought of Mother shrieking for us to run.

The taste of blood on my breath, how guilty I felt as we ran.

'Who showed how meadow grass might take the worm from your cow…'

How they laughed, circled her like dogs, like she was that cow, sick and lost.

'And for that… Does it seem as right… that her life, that your Alice's life, that others' lives should be so spilled?'

I whispered, for if I shouted, I would cry. 'Well, does it?'

The fire hissed, and the rain ran heavy upon the house.

'No.' Croake watched me as I shook. 'But it will not bring back my Alice neither.'

His good eye blinked fierce, as we sat, picking memories like magpies at bones.

If Mother had not taught things, perhaps they would not have come. If we had left on the first whisper of hunters. If she had listened to me. If I had listened to her. If. If. If.

'What will you do?'

How many lines his old face had, drawn by the sun and the rain. And there, a scar. I wondered on the knife that made it, and the hand that wielded it.

'You are a woman on your own, with a young 'un.' His eyes fell to Dill, yearning to stroke her head.

'I will find them.'

My voice came from deep in me, where my song for Mother lay wreathed in her blood.

'And then what, child?' Croake said. 'What will you do?'

Child, was I? Fast I leaned, made him flinch, as my words poured from that hole in my heart, and filled his home, every corner, every shadow.

'I will avenge Mother, old man. Till balance is got. Till those that came are dead.'

His eyes grew wide, his mouth gulped to speak.

'What, now, you would stop me, James Croake?'

'There can be none of that in God's land. Don't you see, girl? This is not the time of old. This is the time of God. Only His word, His law will d—'

'I care not for any god.' I spat to the cross above his bed.

Dill lifted her arm around Berry, who opened a glint of an eye. Gods and dogs.

'Girl!' Croake whispered harsh. 'They will kill you before you strike any balance, or as to seek it. I know they will kill you. And then they will kill others. They will come for our families again! I know they will come. They told me—'

He stopped.

I had him, snared like a rabbit. The rain drummed upon his roof.

I stood slow. '*They* told you what?'

His eyes flew to the window.

'You know these men… don't you?'

He shook his lying head.

I would draw it from him. How?

I looked around, to the hearth I sat on. Something about ash. I had stopped listening to Mother, bored by her spells. Yet there was a song she sang that came to me then.

Ash and fire and stone and ash,
from ash we rise, to ash we go.

She never showed me how to hex. Said she would not till I knew how to heal. But Croake didn't know a hex from a heifer. So, I would play the dark witch, give him a fright.

I took up ash, smoothed it to my fingers.

'What... What are you doing, girl?' Croake stammered.

'You know what I am doing, old man.' I made my voice bold as I spoke Mother's words, 'Ash and fire and stone and ash.'

I wanted to laugh as I watched him shake. I had power over him. It felt good. Better than pain.

'Tell me, who are these men that killed my mother?'

'I...'

'They pissed on her, did you know that?'

'No...'

'And they broke her arm. Do you know what that feels like?'

'Stop.'

But I would not. I spoke the words again, made this hex mine,

'*From ash we rise, to ash we go.*'

'Please, please... I know only some of them. Sons of fathers...'

'Tell me the names of their fathers.' I shook and it seemed the room shook with me.

I took up more ash and let it fall gently. I pressed my toe to it and, with a cut of my foot, drew the ash to point at Croake. Fear came fast to him. His hands were on his belt. Did he mean to pull a knife? His mouth opened and closed. Stupid old man.

'Please... I gave you shelter...'

'Tell me the names,' I seethed, hot as his fire.

I raised my foot above the hex, a blade ready to strike. Croake looked again to the window.

'Why do you look there? You think you trap me, don't you?'

He shook his head.

'Tell me, you... you old fool.'

And I did laugh then. Like when I goaded Dill. I could not help it. But I didn't care.

My laugh cut him, made his tears run.

'It is true... I am a fool...' And I sneered to watch him drop to his shaking knees.

'What is happening? Evey?'

Dill was rubbing her eyes. She rose, looking to me, to Croake, to the ash all about.

'What...? What are you doing?'

'I'm hexing, Dill. Did I do it right?' I swung my words at her.

'No. Stop it, Evey!'

'Go on, old man!' I stood over him. My heart was beating so fast.

He fumbled to his belt. 'They said they would not harm her, if I told them...' And he brought something slowly, but it was not a knife. It was a raggy doll, that shook in his paws.

'If I told them, if I said where to find you, they said they would not hurt her. And so I did. I told them.

'But Alice raged at them, that she loved your mother for her learning from her, and she wouldn't stop her shouting. And so they took her... And... they hung her from the tree.'

Croake threw his hands to his face.

'Now I cannot stop... for seeing her swing there! My Alice! Oh, my Alice!'

My hair rose upon my neck to see him sob before that watching window. He was old, yet he cried like the babe he had lost.

I saw a little girl, blonde and bonny running into the night.

'Alice, I'm sorry,' he whispered.

Dill moved to cradle his head. And as he sobbed to be held, she glared to me.

I looked down to my ashen foot, like it was not

mine. I felt my chest so tight, heat upon my cheeks. I had done this.

I bent and blew into the ash. My hex that was not a hex was no more.

'There were five, but only two I know... Meakin from town. Cooper from across the valley. Army folk. And a lad, not much older than you.' He sniffed. 'Tom, they called him. A wicked lad.'

I watched as Dill fetched a flagon of water.

'They have a leader. A tall one.'

I thought on that man, dropping his arm to loose his dogs.

Croake nodded, as Dill helped him to drink. How good she was. How bad I was.

'That is only four men, Jim Croake.' I could not hex, yet I could count.

'The fifth was a woman, an old woman. She led them here.' Water dribbled from his chin. 'She knew your mother...'

Chill down my spine, like the water from his flagon.

'What did she look like? Tell me!' Dill stayed my hand.

'She was crooked of back. She wore a hood, I did not see her face! I did not see!'

Gently Dill pressed him the doll.

'That's all I know,' and Croake stroked its woollen hair. 'That's all...'

Ash trickled from my fingers.

'Thank you, James Croake.'

He shuffled to his room. He looked to Dill, and she smiled. But he said nothing more, as he passed me, and closed his door.

The rain came down the harder, as the fire shrank to sleep.

Dill put down the flagon, not looking to me. She moved to Berry and her pups.

'It had to be done, Dill.'

My mouth was dry. But no water was offered to the wicked sister.

'Do you not see that?'

She turned and drew the dogs closer to her, further from me.

'Ash is not for hexing, Evey. It is for binding.' She whispered, yet how she stung me.

'I don't care, Dill! I have their names, don't I? I don't care about your spells! I don't care, you hear?'

And yet I knew what stung me more. Part of me, hidden away, did care. To ask her of Mother's words, everything I had stopped listening to.

'I'm happy for you, Evey.'

'Stupid, ungrateful mite! For me? For Mother you should be—'

But I could speak no more.

Dill turned. Her eyes were wet.

'I'm sorry, Evey,' she whispered, 'that you're sad. I miss her too.'

And I did not soothe her as she cried herself to sleep, and the rain dripped her words.

I'm happy for you.

She was too young to understand. But tomorrow she would have to. Tomorrow.

Meakin. Cooper. Tom. Tall One.

I had their names, to make good my promise. And now I must swear to another, beyond the window, swinging ever in the wind. A ghost for an old man who I had called a fool.

Then it came up through me like a wave, and I could not stop it, only hold to the hearth shaking, shaking, stopping my mouth to keep those sobs from filling the room.

'I'm sorry too. I'm sorry, Alice Croake.'

I took Croake's blanket from his empty chair.

I had no more spells to make up. No one left to hurt. Nothing to bring the lost to the hearth where I lay.

Only ash on my fingers, where my tears dropped like little footsteps in the snow.

4

I woke to the smell of burned wood and dust and waited for the *tap tap* of Mother's stick as she limped to stir the embers.

Then I saw a scythe above a door that was not ours, and I remembered.

I had mocked a hex I had never learned, frightened an old man with a pile of ash, and goaded my sister who told me to stop.

Berry groaned, her pups mewling for her milk. Dill opened her eyes. She smiled and it was like day breaking. Though we had quarrelled in the night, she was happy in the morn. That was then, this was now. And I needed her happy this day that must be done.

I stretched to stand and Berry growled.

'Hush, Berry dog.'

I had not seen Croake sitting like a sack by the hearth. He nodded to the table, where bread and cheese waited.

'See...!' said Dill. 'You like her new name!'

My hands sought the food, hoarding to my mouth as squirrels for winter.

Dill pointed, her cheeks full to bursting.

'Can we... take us one, Jim Croake?'

He looked over to those clamouring pups and nodded again. Dill spat cheese.

'Oh, Evey! I'll look to it! I will so! It will be no trouble!'

'No, Dill, another babe will pull us back.'

'I am nine years tall. I am no babe and I do promise—'

'No. It's ever pups and play with you. We have far to go to make the coven by night.'

She fell quiet then, full of temper, tossing gobbets to Berry.

'Come, Dill.' I pulled our bag and rose from the table.

'No. I'm stayin'.'

She dropped her head, hair across her eyes, but I knew their sullen shape.

'Dill, we must away. The day is risen...'

'Then go to it,' she said quiet. 'I want a pup.'

'Dill. Now, I say.'

But I did not have Mother's voice, her tongue stinging as a whip if I crossed her.

So Dill crept to Berry and whispered to her. The dog licked Dill's hand as she plucked a pup with a patched eye from its tussling kin. She fixed me a look and her eyes shone fierce. I remembered in the night, how I spoiled to fight her.

'And I say, now I have a pup, Evey. And that's that.'

Then the pup caught her waving fingers, like a fly trapped in her jaws.

'Ow!' Dill sucked her hand. 'Ow! You weasel!'

Croake laughed out and smacked his old hands upon the hearth, and laughter came to me. I breathed it in the flying dust, and Dill laughed too, wagging her bitten finger to the pup, and I saw Mother in her face and I was happy and sad at once.

'So be it, Dill. You will have to look to it though, else it will die most likes.'

Dill gave a shrug.

'We all die, Evey.'

She jumped her fingers across that pup's jaws, mouthing to catch those pesky things.

'Don't we, my sweet? Yes, we do. I will, and you will, and Evey will...'

'Dill, enough!'

Her sing-song ways. Soon I would not need to hear them. I opened the door, and morning air rushed in, the smell of rain on grass. Outside was all grey light.

'I will call you... Spring!'

And so named, Spring barked. Dill turned to the old man.

'Mind you name the rest now, or I'll be back!' She brought the pup to her cheek. 'Thank you, Jim Croake!'

She was happy, and not to be stopped, life nipping at her heels. One moment a child she was, another older than her years she seemed. I had not thought to thank the old man, who bent for his raggy doll in the dust.

'Come on, Evey! Spring wants to see the world!'

Dill ran from the yard, her pup yapping with glee.

The tree creaked and I thought of when we played in our wood, climbing high as we dared, Mother reaching to guide our toes. Then I saw not us, but Alice who Mother lifted down so gentle, kissing her still cheek.

A fresh wind chased across the valley.

'Eveyyyy!'

Dill was above the farm, climbing into the day.

The tree stood empty. The door closed.

I turned and I followed her, and I never came back to Croake Farm.

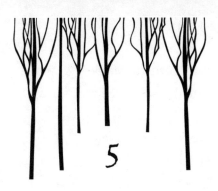

5

The wind moaned as we made towards the ridge. My legs ached from the climb, and from the running. Fear makes you faster.

Dill ran on with Spring, showing her all there was to see under the great sky. Two pups now weighed my skirt. We had to make the coven by nightfall. It would be better then, better for all.

We climbed on and up, heads down, and made for a brace of trees tilted by the wind.

Dill hopped that last to claim her perch and crow to the land below. She stopped and shouted back to me, her words blown away.

'Not far, I told you!'

But Dill only shook her head and shouted again. Sighing, I climbed to her side, where the wind came rushing, and then I saw what she saw.

They were across the valley, galloping fast. I pulled Dill low. Flint stones moved at my fingers. I counted them out.

Meakin from town. Cooper from across the valley. Tom, a wicked lad…

One burly who broke Mother's arm. One thin who pissed upon her. One younger who smashed her skull.

They have a leader. A tall one.

I marked his black hat, proud of his pack.

'It's them, ain't it, Evey?'

'If that beast howls we are got.'

'She don't howl.' Dill stroked the wind through Spring's fur. 'Do you? Evey is a silly sister to think so. Yes, she is…'

'Do you think of nothing but that stupid pup?'

Dill only stared ahead. That made me crosser.

'These men killed Mother—'

'I knows it, Evey.'

'If you're not whispering to a dog, it's that stupid stone—'

'It's not stupid. It's Mother's, and I promised—'

I grabbed her.

'Look at me, will you—'

'Leave me be—'

Sudden a bird cried through our quarrel, swooped out above the ridge.

It was a hawk lifting, searching.

The riders looked up to this hunter as it dropped to the valley.

'Get lower, Dill!' Pebbles slipped under our feet.

We all watched that lord of the air as he frowned upon us.

'What is it, Evey? You know the birds...'

'Goshawk. See, his pale crown...'

'Ah, he's beautiful.'

That he was, as he furled the cloak of his speckled wings, and fell, as an arrow straight and silent to the land. Where a rabbit broke, and leaped this way and that, jumping, jumping, jumping. In a plunge of wings and beak and talons, the hawk struck. If there was a last cry, it was lost on the wind, like that rabbit he lifted up, away into the white sky.

And as we watched from high and below, the hunted, the hunter, I felt a pull in my heart, a song for my tender prey.

'Mark me, Tall One, think you are the hawk?
Nay, you are the rabbit spied from far above.
Run quick, Tall One, run ahead and see.
Think your beak is sharp, my love?
Nay, Tall One, not as sharp as me.'

And like the hawk, I watched him, as he raised to rally his pack. They kicked on, one behind the other, like black ants across the earth.

So I opened my fingers, and I squashed them tight in my sight.

6

'I knows what you're thinking on, Evey.'

I started. I had forgotten Dill. She lay flat to the wind, Spring against her chest.

'I do hate them too.' She bit her lip, looking to that distant pack, now specks of dirt.

How I wanted after them.

'Come on.' I swung my bag for leaving. 'They are gone, we must hurry.'

Dill sighed and all slovenly she pulled herself to.

'How far is it, Evey Bird?'

'Don't call me that!' I said, smarting to her sing-song name.

She sighed again as the wind pulled at Spring's ears. 'Sorry, Evey...'

Slow I pulled them on and slow we began the climb down. Away over the next hill I saw it, a thick furrow of trees. The coven's wood.

The wind came pushing, and we leaned into it like little boats upon a great green wave. The hills rose and fell into the distance. Beyond them I knew was the sea. I had only seen it once, a memory more like a dream. Mother hugging me, baby Dill griping. Cold spray, salt on my face. Then like they flew from my thoughts, a flock of gulls came crying over the rise, circling and banking above us. Ever on the beady take are gulls, haunted by the hunger of their young.

'Do you remember the gull with Mother that day?'

I did. And I could not hide my smile from her.

'You had to fall to the ground for it divin' down...'

I saw it so clear. Us all upon a hill like the one we climbed now. Mother telling us what we should know about the land. She had brought a roll of food. And when we stopped to eat, a gull came, a plummet from the blue, stole the loaf from her hand, and laughed clean away.

'She was fair angry, weren't she, Evey?' Dill held to me.

'Come back, you thief!' I cried, shaking Mother's fist. 'You sea monster!'

'You sky rat!' we said together.

Dill held her stomach for aching as we stumbled on, beneath those crying gulls who seemed to laugh with us. Till we fell to silence. Remembering.

Higher the sun climbed, as the hill swelled behind us and we were in the valley.

'Was it a gull you saw that time?'

I knew straight as anything what she went for. That time.

'No, Dill. It were not.'

'Was it,' she smiled for this game she loved to play, 'a robin puffed and proud?'

I let her pull me. For it would make her come faster, would it not?

'No, Dill.'

'Was it... a brown sparrow searching for his dear love?'

'No, Dill. It were not.'

'Was it... a chough coughing in the trees?'

I breathed in the sky, where the clouds cosseted the sun.

'No, Dill. It were not.'

'Was it... a raven digging for your soul?'

'No, Dill.'

'A heron, that grey king of the river?'

'No.'

'A falcon, proud lord of the hunt?'

'No,' I said, and looked towards that furrow of trees coming closer. I turned to her, to say the words proper. 'Now, only one more bird you may roost.'

Dill squinted. This game, we had played so many years. We played it in the dark, falling to sleep. We played it sitting in the high trees, watching the leaves turn in the light. It was the game she liked best of all.

'Was it… an owl, that white lady of the night?'

I nodded. And Dill nodded.

'Tell me of it, my sister.'

I looked to the listening clouds. And I shivered, for I knew something that she did not. But it was best, she would see that. In time she would.

It had been a few years since I walked this way with Mother. Then, hiding at the foot of the hill, I saw a nestle of trees I remembered, and I knew we were close.

'If I tell you, Dill, will you walk quicker for me?'

'Yes, Evey B—' She caught my eye. 'Yes, Evey, I do swear it, if you tell me.'

The wind breathed Mother's words.

Swear you will look to her. Swear it, Evey.

And I had an idea. How I might keep my promise to look to Dill, and to do what I must without her. I felt the hot quickness of it as it sprang from my tongue.

'When we get to the coven, you will be good and do what you are told?'

'Ouch! Little monster!' Dill pulled Spring from her hair.

I walked faster, and so caught, she ran to catch me.

'Evey, please! Finish the story!'

'Swear it first, Dill. "I will be good and do what I am told."'

Swear it, Evey.

I swallowed. I am keeping my oath, Mother.

'We, Dill and Spring, do swear to you, Evey, that we will be good and do what we are told! Now, tell it, Evey! Tell it! I did swear!' she cried, and Spring barked to join her.

I slowed, letting her tug to my side. My idea burned upon my cheeks.

Rising from the wood ahead, a rook took wing, a blade opening.

Dill took my hand. 'Please tell me about the owl, Evey. Like Mother used to tell it.'

Her smile twitched. She did not know what she swore for, but it was best.

'I was a little 'un. Much littler than you…'

'Red of hair and rushing at the world, that's what Mother said you were.'

'So I was, Dill.'

'It was sunset, Evey…' I felt the eager pull of her hand.

'It was sunset,' I said. 'And the sky was so gold and beautiful in that ploughed field, like it shone upon a great brown sea. And I was running ahead of Mother who laughed to watch me and told me, "Run on, run on, little Evey Red Braid." And I did, glad to be free, yet knowing Mother was there, and I jumped on through the sun's lowering light.'

I watched as another rook cut the air.

'And as I danced to catch my shadow along those furrows, I heard something behind me, and I turned quick, and stopped my breath...'

Dill's hand grew tighter.

'It was a great white owl perched upon a broken tree, as if she sat upon a throne. And the setting sun shone through her eyes of amber, that she turned upon me. In her golden court, her beak was so black, her talons were so long, and her wings were...'

'White as whispered snow,' whispered Dill, as she put her head to my shoulder.

Another croak. Another rook. They knew we came closer.

'That great owl opened her beak and it was like she was speaking only to me.'

'What did she say, Evey?'

'She called my name, Dill, soft and straight, over, and over, "*Evey, Evey, Evey.*" And I was so pleased that I bowed to her, and saw that she bowed too, bobbing her beautiful head, her round eyes fixed upon me.'

'And what did Mother do, Evey?'

'She kneeled down in the field, and so I did same. I pressed my knees to the mud, and I could not help my delight, as I pointed and cried, "Queen! Queen! Queen!"

'And as my laugh flowed across the field, that queen lifted into the sun and she flew towards me, all wings and eyes, a rush of white across my head. But I wasn't afeared, as I felt her feathers brush my cheeks, her talons stroke. I only turned to watch her go and saw that she had plucked a lock of my red hair, for it caught the sunlight like a flame. I watched her as she rose, black against the light, and with last a cry, "*Evey*," she swooped beyond the field, and was gone.'

'And what did Mother see, Evey?'

I felt my head, tracing the scar under my hair.

'She saw where the owl had touched me. It was not deep. It did not hurt. Though I remember my heart beat fast to see my blood upon her finger.'

'And what did Mother say?'

'She said…'

Again I shivered. It was colder, and the woods were waiting. The rooks cawed. But only I could hear them.

'Mother said it was my naming. For that queen had marked me so and taken my hair as a token. Now I would be one with her kind, could call on them, would know their words.'

'I wish I had a naming, Evey.'

Spring was asleep in her arms. The rooks chuckled.

'You will, Dill. You will soon.'

'Finish the story, Evey. Tell me what Mother said last of all.'

I drew her on, towards those woods, taller, darker, full of laughter.

'She said, "For you, my little chick, my only crow, my redbreast love, from now and ever always will be, Eveline of the Birds."'

Dill yawned, happy for the end of the story, like she would sink to her bed. The rooks were laughing. But only I knew why.

'What do they say, Evey?'

Liar. Liar. Liar.

I drew her close. 'They say, "Welcome, sisters. This way. This way."'

And lying, I led Dill into the wood.

7

The night sky was clear, cupped by the waning moon, as my memories of that place dropped like pebbles to ripple a pond.

Last time I came with Mother, Dill was but a babe and I was no more than six year. Yet I knew the coven was close. Alder and yew stood all about, a crowd of tall shadows. And we heard nor smelled no beast. For witches do love to hunt.

'Why do we come here, Evey?'

Spring whined upon Dill's shoulder.

'Have I not told you enough, Dilly?'

I stumbled in the dark, where a branch snapped. They would hear that right enough.

'Tell me again, Evey Bird—'

'Don't call me that! You know as well as I. Because it was Mother's wish! Because we need help! "Get to the coven. Find my sister," she said. Because we must do what she wanted, and not keep asking why!'

Dill dragged her feet. She was tired. I was tired of her.

I felt a pull in my belly. *Look to Dill.* Like Mother jabbed me for what I had not said.

'I can hear...' Dill stopped. 'Singing.'

We listened among those tall bodies of blue and black and grey. Then slight, then stronger came the sound of voices twisting through the branches. We were too far to hear what they sang. It was the coven for sure. For witches do love to sing.

'Come on, we are close...'

But Dill pulled me back.

'Dilly! We are going there. You swore to m—'

'No, Evey, look!'

A shape came on through the trees.

Its white hands like gloves, hair long to its waist, as a blanket of silver threads.

Dill drew behind me. Silence, but for those singers, weaving their words.

'Evey, what is that?'

'Shhh...'

I would not be afeared, yet I felt my heart hammer so hard it might echo among those trees.

'I... I am...'

'Eveline of the Birds.'

Her voice filled the darkness. I could not see her lips. She was a shroud, floating above the ground.

'Just Eveline.'

The woman looked down to us like one of the trees of the forest, tall and pale and still. Her face was narrow. Her eyes as a raven's, sharp and quick. And I knew her then. She was my Aunt Grey.

'And you must be little Dill.'

Grey bent to her. Spring growled.

'Just Dill.' I knew she was sullen for that 'little'. 'Who are you, please?'

The witch laughed. It was a sound like the turning of dry leaves.

'Ah, little Dill, it is good to see you.'

She stepped closer, and I smelled lavender, wood bark, smoke. She stretched out her hands, as a silver birch springing to life, her hair flowing forward like to touch us.

'You were but a babe when I saw you last.'

Another pebble dropped into the pool of my memory. A great fireside with Mother, the witches passing Dill from one to other. Dill stretching for Mother's arms, crying as the witches kissed her. Me weighed with sleep. Mother and Grey talking close. Grey laughing. Mother frowning. And then nothing more, ripples run to still.

Grey kneeled. 'I know what it is to be a younger sister. I am Grey. Your aunt.'

She reached to stroke Dill's cheek. Spring barked.

Grey laughed again, and again that sound of leaves rustling.

'Greetings, little pup.'

She stood, and turned her eyes to me, like Mother's but not Mother's.

'Eveline – is my sister come?'

It was like an arrow to my heart, piercing right through.

For a moment I could bring no words, as my aunt looked out to the darkness. For a moment, I listened for the sound of her staff striking the trees, her scolding me and Dill for running on. For a moment I thought she was come and would step smiling to our midst and greet her sister.

'She's dead.'

Dill's voice was hard like her hand.

Grey grasped my wrist.

'When?'

'A day gone. Men came. Hunters.' My voice fell like a dead chick in that wood. I began to shake and Grey was about me, folding me to her, holding me close, and I could smell that scent of lavender and smoke, as she whispered to my ear,

'They will never take her spirit. You know that, don't you?'

I tried to nod, my head too tight to her shoulder, her long hair across my cheek.

'Oh, my sister, my sister, our ways were different, but you were my blood always and ever…' She stroked my head. 'You poor little things.'

And she pulled Dill too, I heard her gasp as tighter Grey held us, with a *shhh* and a *shush, now*, like we were babes in the crib. It was strange. I did not know my aunt good, but she smoothed my hair like Mother used to, till I made her stop, for I felt too old for it, and now this woman who was both family and a stranger did it, and I wanted to cry and be comforted and told it would be all right, but also I wanted to push away her smell, her pulling arms, her voice like old leaves.

'Come now, my sister's children.' Grey felt our faces. 'Follow me.'

She turned, and walked between the trees, floating slow through the gloom.

I had to talk to the coven, tell them of Mother, of Tall One, his pack. I looked to Dill. I needed them to help me.

'Evey, I'm not sure—'

'Dill, are you hungry?'

'Yes, but—'

'Are you tired?'

That jab again at my belly.

'And what of poor Spring? Your pup needs food.'

'But, Evey, I am frightened.'

She pressed her face to Spring, breathing in her whimpers.

Grey stood still as a tree, watching us. And the singing came again, like they sang only to us, two lost witches in the wood.

'Dill, I promise you, we will rest and then be on our way.'

I swallowed, my mouth was dry with lies.

She stopped her stroking the pup. 'You do promise, Evey?'

The smell of fire came on the air, bringing more of meat and broth. I ached from hunger, ached to sit, but most I ached to get Dill there.

'Promise,' I whispered and reached for her.

And Dill clung gladly to me, as we followed our Aunt Grey, a spirit leading us deeper into the night.

8

'Look, Dilly!'

Flames danced among the trees. And as we drew nearer, the voices grew louder.

'There was a valley,
and in that valley,
was a woman,
of witching way.'

So they sang, so Grey floated on, so those voices led us. Till we made a clearing, where the trees were yellow and red and orange by the light of a great fire.

'She walked the valley,
that witching valley,
that woman of our way.'

We stepped into that light and felt the warmth upon our faces. Around that lusty flame, a ring of witches sat singing over.

'She walked that valley,
that witching woman,
as she made
her witching way...'

The singing stopped. The witches looked to us. Dill's hand gripped tighter to mine. Grey curled her fingers about my shoulder.

'Eveline of the Birds is come to us.'

Only the fire moved.

'With her sister, little Dill.'

The witches stared to Dill, who stared back. I knew she counted them. There would be twelve. For Mother did not sit among them. Still were their faces, some old, some young. Long was their hair, some grey and streaked like a charm of magpies. Strangers all, for I could not recall them. I remembered only the fire and them around it, laughing and talking and singing. Like they had been sitting there ever always, waiting for us.

Grey drew us forward. 'They bring news of my sister,' and those witches all looked to each other, then back to us.

'Eveline, make your tell.'

Silence, but for the simmer of pot, and spit of flame. My belly groaned and my bones cried sleep. And in that watching stillness, Dill turned Spring from her shoulder. The pup yawned, blinking her black eye.

'My...' I looked to Dill. 'Our...'

I swallowed the heat and looked straight at those eyes filled with flames.

'Mother is dead.'

Like water hurled upon their fire, with one mouth they hissed aloud. Some threw their hands to the orange air, some wrung their faces, some sat and stared.

Grey pressed to my shoulder. 'Finish your tell, Eveline.'

'Men... Men came that day...'

Tears clawed my throat, as my words came flooding.

'Witch hunters. Four men. They killed her. I...'

Murmuring and muttering rose, but Grey held her hand for silence.

'Mother told us once that the witching way is... witch blood spilled must be balanced, and that the coven must be asked. So...' I swallowed the pain, 'I have two asks.'

Dill sat, her head down, as she stroked Spring. But I knew she listened true.

'I have their names.'

And I thought of Mother shouting for us to flee.

'First, I ask for blood. For my right. To avenge what they did.'

I closed my eyes to stop from crying. But instead I saw Tall One raise his arm high, like as to hail me. And he let it fall. And his dogs sprang to Mother.

I opened my eyes. My tears had run. I felt numb, as I watched Grey move from my side, to huddle in mutters with her sisters.

Why had I come here? I cared not for their witching way.

But I knew full why. Because of my second ask.

'We hear you, Eveline of the Birds...'

Grey's voice came bold across the flames. That name. How I hated that she used it.

'Your ask is granted. Seek your balance, avenge your mother.'

And then she was hugging me, like she had stepped through the fire itself.

'Hunt them for me,' she whispered close to my ear.

The murmuring of those witches grew louder with shouts of anger and sobs and then the clearing was all hubbub, their shadows across the flickering light.

'My sister was our natural leader...' Her voice sounded through me, and again I smelled sweet lavender.

'She was a good woman, who taught kindness and healing, helping others.'

She stepped back, tracing my hair.

'And she was strong. Like you.'

I could not speak. I nodded.

'Can you find these men?'

I watched Dill, as she lifted Mother's stone from her pocket and murmured to it.

'I can hunt,' I said.

Grey held to my shoulders. 'I believe you can, Eveline.' She motioned. 'Mabel…'

A young witch, all dusky curls, came and sat with Dill. She looked away.

'Tally, bring food,' said Grey to another.

'Is that your mother's scrying stone?' asked Mabel.

She smiled and the fire shone in her round cheeks.

'I like your pup, little Dill.'

Spring sniffed Mabel's fingers. Dill shifted the stone away and drew Spring to her chest. A frown grew across her brow like a weed from a wall.

'She has a way, the little one…'

Mabel laughed, and drew a blanket to my shoulders, as Grey circled the fireside, nodding, gesturing. The coven seemed to bend to her.

'She is tired only.' I looked to my sullen sister, as she picked at the ground.

'Here, young 'uns. Tally made it good and hot.'

Her hands, bent and bony, held a bowl each. Two teeth glinted beneath her hood.

'It will make your hair curl, like Mabel's.' She laughed like a branch cracking.

I grabbed that bowl right quick. It steamed full of food and warmth.

'I don't want no curls.' Dill shook her head.

'Oh, now…' Mabel went to stroke her. 'Such a shame, they would suit you.'

Dill hunched away, only stroking her dog and the stone.

'Dill, please.'

She buried her head to her knees.

'I'm sorry for her. Thank you.'

I took Dill's bowl from Tally's wrinkled fingers.

'We drink to our sister, lost to us.'

Grey lifted her own to the flicking, spitting air. And those witches lifted same.

'Lost to us… Lost to us…'

The coven settled, supping in silence.

All but Dill.

I could feel Grey's eyes upon us, watching through the fire.

'Dilly, I know you are hungry,' I whispered. 'And did you not swear to be good?'

Dill looked to me, not tired nor churlish, just sad.

'I'm sorry, Evey.' She twisted her fingers in Spring's fur. 'I miss Mother so and the broth minded me of her.'

'Then do it for Mother. Please, Dill.'

Slow she took the bowl from me and lifted it to her trembling mouth.

My belly twisted for what was coming. So quick I drowned it, sank into the steam and drank and lapped and gobbled. I felt good as that broth ran warm about my body, sank me to a hot darkness that—

'What is your second ask, Eveline of the Birds?'

Grey's voice came across the clearing, through my raised bowl.

She had come to it, and I must face it.

All looked to me, and Grey smiled through the flames, and Dill hummed as she lifted scraps to Spring who bolted them down.

'Ask it, Eveline,' said Grey. 'Do not be afeared. Are we not family?'

I wormed gristle from my teeth. They were no family I knew, yet I needed them. Mother said Grey would protect us. And Grey had brought me to it. So it was time.

'I ask that...' I must just say it. 'That the coven look to my sister.'

Dill stopped her humming and turned to me.

'Look to little Dill?'

'Yes.' I swallowed that fat, cold and slimy in my mouth. 'Alone I must seek the men who killed Mother.'

'Evey?' Dill's eyes were so wide to me. 'What do you mean?'

Grey rose and moved along the fireside, Mabel and Tally following.

'Dill, it is too dangerous.' My belly twisted. But this was best. 'You know I cannot take you.'

She stood, spilling her bowl for Spring to lap.

'No, Evey! I do not know! I do not know!'

She pointed at me, jabbing the air with her fist round the stone.

'I will not stay here! You promised we—'

'Little Dill.' Grey was close. 'You will be safe with us.'

Dill slapped Grey's hand away.

'Stop calling me that!'

Dill stepped back, the stone raised, black in the light.

'Come, we will be sisters all!' said Mabel.

'No, we won't!'

And now she struck away Mabel's hand.

'Dilly.' I moved to her. She was panicked I could see.

'Ah!' cried Mabel. 'How she bites!'

And the coven laughed and Dill glared.

'Dilly, calm down.'

'She won't bite old Tally!'

Darting in, the old witch hooked her bony fingers under Dill's arms.

'Dill, please…'

'Not if she's tickled!'

'Leave! Me! Be!'

Dill swung her fist wild, and the stone struck Tally, blood gushing from her cheek.

The old witch cried and fell to her knees. The coven gasped as one.

'Dill!'

'I did not mean to do it!'

'Look what you did!'

Mabel pressed her shawl to Tally's wound.

'I forgot the stone was in my hand. I'm sorry, old lady, you surprised—'

'Give me that!'

I wrenched it from Dill's grasp.

'Shame that you bring me and Mother!'

'Evey, no! Please! You mustn't!'

'No, Dill!' I held the stone from her reach. 'You are not to have it, you hear?'

'But, Evey! Mother said it should be only given or found, never taken… Never taken.' She sobbed to breathe. 'You don't… don't know.'

She jumped to claw my hand, Spring barking over.

'Oh, I don't know?' I pushed her away. 'I don't have your gift. Is that it?'

I held the stone high from Dill and her damn dog.

'No, Evey! No!'

I wanted to laugh as she jumped to reach my hand.

'You swore to be good!'

And then I saw Mabel and another young witch creep slow behind Dill.

'The stone is not yours! It was Mother's and I am the eldest, so...'

'No, Evey, please, it's not like that.'

'Always you have played with it and whispered to it. You think I do not see?'

'Evey, listen—'

'You listen for once!' I grabbed her. 'You think you're better than me?'

'No! No! You're hurting me!'

Dill shook her head, trembling as the coven watched.

'Well, I've had enough, Dill.' I pushed her thin shoulder, made her stumble. I had never done that. But she made me so cross. 'Mother's gifted favourite can stay here and learn from the witches!'

'I do not want to, Evey! I want to be—'

'I don't care!' Spit on my lip. 'You will do as you are told! You swore!'

Dill fell to her knees, begging through her tears. And I swallowed hard. For my spite grew bitter as I watched her.

'She will soften, Evey.' Grey was there, pressing a bag to me. 'For the road.'

'Hush, little one, we will not hurt you,' said Mabel, and circled her arms to Dill.

'No!' Dill turned about.

'Calm now, calm…' said that other witch, her voice and black hair flowing, as an otter slipping through water. 'What a fuss for one so little.'

'Go away! Get off me!'

I swallowed harder, to watch Dill struggle against Mabel's arms and this otter girl, all sharp smile. It felt like I was in another's body as I weighed the stone in my hand, swung the bag on my shoulder. Like my arms and legs moved without me knowing.

'Come, Eveline, I will show you the way.'

And Grey led me past Dill, writhing and pushing to get free of those girls.

'I will give it to you! Don't leave me here! Please, I will give the stone to you!'

And though the hairs on my neck rose at her cry, a laugh grew inside me, and I waved my hand to tease her.

'But, sister, I have it already.'

I winked to her white face gaping.

'And you will be safe here. I told you that.'

'Evey, why are you doing this? I don't like them! I don't like her! She stinks… like dead flowers! I don't like—'

'Enough, child!' Grey's voice cracked across the fireside. 'You will stay, and you will learn respect, daughter of my sister.'

She towered sudden across the fire, her hair twining with the dancing flames.

'Evey! Evey!'

'I will come back, Dill. I will.'

But even as I said those words, did I know if I would?

Grey pulled me on. We passed heads nodding, hands reaching.

'Mother!'

I swallowed hardest then.

And though I knew I shouldn't, I felt glad as Dill's voice grew further away, for it pained me to hear her.

'Mother!'

Grey's long fingers were upon my back. And the witches began to sing again, so that Dill's cries joined their voices.

'…other!'

She would calm. She would understand in time. I looked to the stone, turning it in the glow from the fire behind us and the shadows of the trees.

'You were right to take it, Eveline.'

Grey moved to stroke my hand. I felt her breathing next to me. That sweet smell. Like dead flowers, Dill called it.

'Was I? I do not know. I never listened to Mother. Dill… Dill did.'

'This stone is not for little girls. It can be a powerful weapon, Evey. Blood magick.'

I looked up to her. Black eyes blacker in the moving dark.

'A weapon? Mother never said.'

Grey nodded, her shape shifting. 'When Dill struck Tally, it woke at the taste of her.'

The stone sudden seemed alive in my hand.

'And now it is hungry, Evey. Give the stone all your anger, and it will make you strong. Feed it the blood of your enemies. Our enemies.'

And her fingers closed mine about the stone as the witches' song filled the air.

'Seek your revenge. Hunt them all. For your mother. For me.'

She kissed my cheek.

'Follow the river west. The road to town lies through the woods. There, you will find your balance, Eveline of the Birds.'

'I will find them.'

I placed the stone into the bag. Again came that feeling, that I placed a creature to my side. I looked back to the fire where Dill would be crying and struggling to follow.

'My sister doesn't understand... but I must do this alone.'

Grey smiled, became like one of those silver birch again.

'She is only little. Go now.'

And she watched me step through the branches, cold earth beneath my toes. I moved from the last of light into the darkness, the witches' words growing fainter and fainter.

'She walked the valley,
that witching valley,
that woman of our way.'

Till I could hear them no more. And Dill's cries no more.

And I was alone at last.

And free.

9

It was dawn light when I stopped.

My body ached so. I had not wanted sleep.

The path was sheer with large stones that tumbled away. I remembered them scattering under my feet in the dark. I stood on the rise, an elm stretching its great green arms above me.

A pair of fat pigeons preened and fluttered against the branches. *Are you lost, Eveline? Are you? Are you?*

I looked to the woods below.

'I don't know.'

Flutter, flutter. *Can we help? Can we? Can we?*

I sat to open the bag from Grey and closer the pigeon sisters cooed, *What have you there? Tasty treats?*

Apples and nuts, some dry meat, bread, a gourd of water. But I did not want to eat. Dill's cries for Mother stayed my hunger. I picked at the bread, thinking on my sister's pale face. I had been so hard towards her last night, that feeling of not being in my body. But it was for her own good. It had to be.

I threw morsels for those begging birds, and they fell to them.

Thank you, oh, thank you, kind sister.

They gobbled and trilled, before they hefted up, and winged across the rocky path to the woods.

Follow! Follow! We know! We know!

I tried to stand but want had ebbed from my limbs. I reached for the gourd and felt something hard and smooth to my fingertips.

Mother's scrying stone.

I took it out, turning it upon my palm. Jet as a moonless night. Tiny glints of light. And there a notch, like a thumbnail pressed to its hard skin. I rubbed it, thinking on the words of my Aunt Grey.

You were right to take it, Eveline.

I had snatched it from Dill. But she was waving it so. Hurt that old witch.

Shards of light turning, like stars. There was something she cried, something...

Mother said it should only be given or found, never taken!

Stones were everywhere about me. Though none as fine as the one in my hand.

It rolled smooth on my palm. Tally bled where Dill hit her. Stupid, jealous mite.

It woke at the taste of her.

I watched those black stars turning in my hand.

Blood magick.

I didn't know no magick. Dill did. Mother did. Had. Dill's face. Sobbing.

I have the stone already, little Dill.

My voice outside me, laughing at her.

But Mother was dead, so she couldn't stop me.

She was only little. *Little Dill.* Shouldn't have teased her.

And I was drifting in those stars. I couldn't help it. Mother was dead.

My eyes so heavy. So tired, so tired, so…

You screamed. I wrestled to be free.

Pain in my sides held tight. I heard bodies moving, murmuring.

'Is this the one you spoke of, old woman?'

'This is her, sire. A dark witch taken shape of a child.'

I smelled their horses, pawing the earth.

Felt heat from a fire, shadows of flames.

'Bind her mouth before she curses our souls!'

'No, leave me be! Leave me be!'

'Hold still, devil!'

You shrieked till a blond boy shut your mouth. As a burly man bound you. A thin one slung you to his horse, while a tall one watched on.

'Spells aplenty she cast, as was bid...' the old woman croaked. 'Against your king, who hides weak and beaten...'

'None shall know of it. We are done here, woman.'

I wriggled so hard, whimpered so loud.

'Hush, pretty one...' A young girl, her curls on my face.

'Aye,' cracked a crone. 'Or I will bite your tail.'

Her toothless smile. Her blade to my cheek.

'Look now!' laughed the girl. 'Look at John Barrow the bear. How drunk he is!'

A great man kicked the fire, sprayed sparks to the night. His head was a bear. A mask that bellowed and drank.

You looked to me, bound and mute.

The horses reared. You kicked and kicked.

No. Please.

A hand on my neck, lifted me high.

'Ah, do you want her?'

Yes. Yes, so much.

'Then fly!'

And flung me.

Don't cry, I am coming. Like those birds we love to chase.

I flew into the flames and the heat and the light.

I howled, for you were not there.

So alone, I burned for you.

IO

'**N**o!'

  I scrambled to my feet, looking to beat the flames. My foot twisted and I fell, a rock biting.

I breathed, my knee pulsing pain. There was no fire. No men, no old woman. It was a stupid dream. Such a strange dream. I remembered I had been looking at Mother's stone...

It was still in my grip. I rubbed the dust from its black face, made those shards shine. Mother would roll it in her palms at a healing as she scryed with it.

A horse whinnied behind me.

Quick I stood, pain up my leg as I moved, shoving the stone to my bag.

A rider was coming down the rocky path.

'Well met there!'

It was a man's voice. And he meant no harm, hailing as friend in this warring time, when a stranger would kill another for king or country. For that I trusted no man, no matter what he hailed.

The path below ran down into the shadow of the forest. If this man was a wolf, then I would not be in open sight.

'Hey! Hey, stop!'

When Mother and I hunted it was always under shelter, staying low, moving quick and silent through the trees.

'Be not afeared! Well met, I say!'

His horse spurred, stones rolling beneath its hooves. I stepped quicker still. The path became thinner, and the trees reached up from a drop to my side. The air was wet. A river chattered far below.

'Please stop!' Closer came the jangle of stirrup and bit.

His horse snorted. I shivered in the shade. I had no weapon.

'Mistress, I mean no harm!'

From a bend in the steep path, where the green light grew darker, came another horse's snort. Was this the witch hunters penning me like a lamb for slaughter? Well, I would face these wolves, and show them my own teeth.

The sound of the river trickled through the air. The horse blew close to my ear and I moved to the drop.

Behind me, I felt the heat from its great body fill that narrow way.

'Ah, at last...'

I looked up, the sunlight through the leaves blinding me. His shape against the sun moved to touch his forelock.

'I have reached you, mistress.'

And there was a strange weight, a warmth on that word *mistress*. I kept moving, sliding my feet across the skittering stones. One jumped and fell to the drop. If I ran, I could not leave the path on my side, the fall would surely kill me.

'Mistress,' he said above the breathing of his horse. 'I am a messenger seeking the Whitaker estate. Do you know it?'

He was wiry, his thin face lined about. A scar upon his chin, and hair like pitch, doused with sweat. And seeing me also, he smiled. He should not have, for his teeth were broken and brown. I shook my head.

'Ah, you are lost too,' his smile widening, 'aren't you, fair maid?'

I felt my cheeks grow hot. I had never been called fair. I had not known men much. A boy once. But I did not like this man, smiling so hungry to me.

'I am... I am not lost.' I could not stop my voice from shuddering. 'I do not know this place you seek.' I looked down. The sun played upon the river, stroking her long back.

The man twisted in his saddle, creaking leather. He leaned to watch me as on I stepped from rock to rock, my feet catching their craggy edges.

'Then you are not from here?'

I did not look to him. 'No, I am not,' rocks kicking, rolling, 'I'm from nowhere.' And it sudden pained me to say this aloud. Home was gone and ahead was nothing. He chuckled, pulling the horse over.

'The girl from nowhere, eh?'

The river laughed beneath the sun's caress. I smelled wet earth upon her bank, sharp garlic spiced the air. And there again, I heard that other horse from the path below. Yet the rider did not for all his creaking and shifting, and his broken smiling.

'So, then, where are you going to, my red-haired pretty?'

Again my cheeks burned. But also from anger. I was alone with this man, this well-met stranger, who pressed to my space upon this empty path, who called me fair and pretty.

We were deeper to the woods, and darker it was. 'I am going to town.' I looked him straight.

He only nodded, as his eyes wandered unbidden over my chest, my waist, my legs. I drew the bag across me, his gaze sudden making me feel shame. Why, though? It was my body, not his.

'Town, is it? That's a long way on foot, my red ruby.' His tongue flicked his teeth. 'Why don't we...'

His horse slipped on a rock, neighing with fright and, as he cursed to draw hard on the reins, I thought who was this man who made me feel so afeared to be a woman?

'Whoa! Steady now...'

His clothes were rough and muddied. A blade was slung sleeping at his side. A soldier messenger, then? His saddlebag showed clothes. A gourd. A blanket.

'Does your mother not worry for you?' He brought the horse to settle. 'Such a lovely, on this road all alone?'

It was not a blanket. I stepped closer to see. The horse snorted.

'No, she does not.' And never would again.

Something about that blanket that was not a blanket.

His thin lips slid over those terrible teeth. 'Oh, but a mother should worry, my little flame...' Pulling his horse to stand.

I reached to that cloth I saw there.

'Ah.' He watched my searching hands. 'You like this?'

And he pulled the blanket free, so that it fell open like a pennant for a family crest. And a great ache flooded my body, as I touched the woven braids, those wood beads I had played with so long, the white thread woven to its edge, like the grey line of her hair. Mother's shawl.

My fingers trembled to feel it, like I smoothed along her still body that had once held me and would no more.

'I was keeping it for a pretty maid.' His voice slid around me. The river laughed on. That smell of garlic so strong. The horse's eye glaring. 'And, my, how right I was to...'

He stank of sweat. His steed smelled better. My fingers dug to Mother's shawl.

'What is your name, sir?'

He smiled to see me tremble.

'Cooper, mistress.' He bent closer. 'James Cooper, at your service.'

Old man Croake's words came tumbling like those stones. *Cooper from across the valley.* And the river caught them and cast them high. *Cooper! Cooper!* she cried.

'And now... I must know yours, my red fox.'

My fingers gripped upon this piece of Mother hanging from his horse.

'Eveline.' My lips twitched, fighting my scream. And he grunted, for he saw his shy maid, tarrying for her kiss.

'Eveline.' He growled to the wet air. 'Ah, Eveline…'

He reached down to my hand, pressed his dirty finger.

'So, my red-haired Eveline, you like this fine shawl?'

How I wanted to bite off that creeping finger, spit it to the river.

'I do, James Cooper. I do, so very much.'

'Really?' He wooed closer. 'And how much do you love it, my red rose?'

His eyes stripped me bare. Bile scalded my throat.

'As much,' I looked up into his laughing eyes, 'as I love my mother.'

His finger stroked to my shaking fist.

'For, you see, James Cooper,' I whispered so that he leaned close. 'It is hers. It is my mother's.' And my lisp was gentle no more. 'Who you killed.'

There was a stillness in that green light. His smile fixed as his eyes filled with knowing. Then right clear, beyond the bend in the path, horse hooves clip-clopped, clip-clopped.

Cooper looked up, and I jumped to. Balling my fist, I wrenched the shawl free.

'You!'

He lunged. I dropped, but his fingers grabbed to my hair.

'I have you!'

I screamed, pulling back, pain across my head, and I ripped away. Like a lover spurned he bellowed and lunged again. I ducked beneath the horse's belly, and I ran down the path, my heart pounding with my feet.

'Stop!'

But I would be wooed by him no more. Mother's shawl in my grasp, I ran on, my scalp singing.

'Ha!'

I turned to see him kick his horse, and it screamed to clatter down upon me. I looked about, the drop to the river was too far.

'I'm coming, my red wench! I'll get you and...'

The turn in the path was closer. Cooper's voice filled the trees, the rocks, the air.

'I'll get you and when I do...'

I made the bend. And there, towering above me was another horse, and upon it sat a young woman, fine and noble, garbed in a long green cloak. I stopped. The rocks skipped around me. The woman looked down to me, with eyes as bright as the sunlit leaves. She began to smile. Was she even there? Was she a wood spirit come to claim me?

With a snort, Cooper's horse rounded the bend,

'I'll take more than your red fur... You...'

He brought his horse fast to stop and stared like me.

'You little...'

His words tumbled to the river below, as the woman looked to Cooper in the dust of that rocky path, and to what he held aloft, like his lady's favour.

A stolen lock of my red hair.

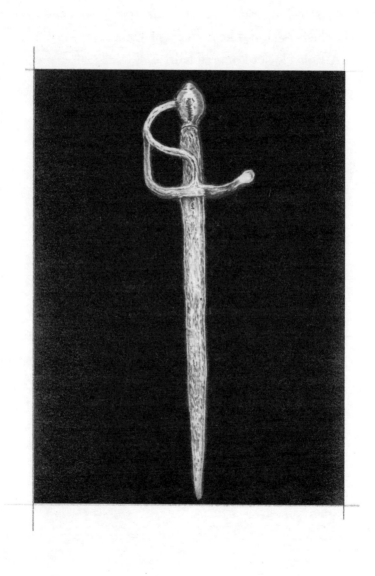

II

We three strangers looked to each other, Cooper to this fine lady, she to him, and I from one to the other. Silence but for Cooper's horse that pawed over.

'Who are you?'

Her voice was soft in that mottled light.

His steed bit to its bridle, eyes wary to its fellow, still as stone.

'I am Cooper, James Cooper...' he said under that woman's steady green gaze. 'Of the town brigade, my lady.'

And Lady Greeneye then alighted to me, my breath as fast as my beating heart.

'And why are you chasing this woman, James Cooper of the town brigade?'

She spoke so clear like day cutting night.

'She stole from me.' Cooper bared his horrid fangs.

The fine lady looked to my hair in his fist.

'And you from her, I see...'

Cooper let fall my lock and it drifted, a red flame in the prying sunlight.

'I could not steal what is not yours to have!' I blurted, like my voice had come from me unbid. Was it this lady who gave me heart?

'Shut your hole, witch!'

'It is not his!' The beads rattled on the shawl as I shook it. 'It was my mother's!'

I pleaded to Greeneye, and she frowned, working our tale between her thoughts. She would know it.

'He is the thief. He ripped it from her dead body!'

The lady looked to Cooper. What a sight we were. Did she think we played to thieve her?

'She was a witch, my lady. Like this one,' and he pointed to me, 'to be brought to trial.'

Lady Greeneye raised an eyebrow. 'Yet she died?'

'She resisted our arrest.' Cooper thrust his chin, like he faced his captain. 'Tried to cast a spell upon us and—'

'That's a lie!' I stepped closer to him and his snorting horse. 'There were four of them. They killed her, like she was a beast to slaughter!'

'And I will kill you, girl, if you dare to speak again!' Cooper drew his blade, scraping the air. 'I arrest you—'

'Stay that sword!' Lady Greeneye rose taller upon her horse which stirred and seemed to grow with her.

'My lady!' He eyed her, stabbed at me. 'Witches are decreed traitors against the people's army! I have my orders!'

'I am aware of your new laws, James Cooper.' Her eyes lit. 'I said stow your blade!'

And that was my moment.

I ran past her silent steed, darting to the path, two, three, four steps away.

'NO!' Cooper raged.

'Stop!' The lady drove before him.

I could have run on then, left them both to tussle horses and argue, but instead I turned and saw Cooper's horse rear, saw him raise that glinting blade to charge at me. He made to pass her with eyes only for me, but Lady Greeneye would not let him. And Cooper stared angry upon this strange woman of the wood, who grit her teeth so wilful to stop him. And then as they scuffled, as their horses jostled, they lost their balance, for neither would give, and together they tumbled and fell, shouting, struggling to the ground.

Cooper's horse reared again, turning tight, the lady's steed trapped beside it, skidding at stones that fell to the river. And beneath those sliding hooves, Cooper and Lady Greeneye heaved and battled.

I had to help. She had saved me, and now grim-faced fought that swinging blade. I started back, scrambling over the rocks.

'You cannot,' Cooper grunted, turning his weight upon her, 'stop me, my lady. Foolish to try.'

Then I saw it in his sweaty grin. We were alone with him upon this path, empty of any traveller. His word against ours. If he killed this brave woman, no one would believe a witch. He would say I killed her.

'I will!' Lady Greeneye's voice echoed above the cry of the horses.

Cooper's steed barged, hemmed by the other, rolled its mad eye.

But Cooper was too heavy upon the lady who shook to hold him fast. I jumped to, grabbed his sword arm. Cooper's other hand gripped mine, and now we three fought to wrestle that sword free.

And his horse slipped, hooves stamping, sliding near.

'I am powered,' sweat from Cooper's brow dripped to her dress, 'by Lord Whitaker himself.'

And then, spite our pulling, he was stronger, for slow he raised his arm, and I saw what he meant to do. To strike his sword pommel upon that lady.

Yet she looked him straight with a smile.

'And I am powered to tell you that I am his daughter!' she hissed, above the cry of his whinnying horse.

'What?' Cooper gaped, as a fish for water. 'His daughter? What?'

I grabbed for the blade. But my hand slipped, and the steel sliced my palm.

'No!'

Cooper punched my face so fast, and I fell back into Greeneye.

He was crazed, for we were laid before him, and such bloodlust foamed his mind.

His horse smashed down its hooves, sparks flew.

'You should not have come this way today.' Cooper raised his blade. 'This path is too dangerous for fine ladies!'

With that he swung back.

And stuck his blade to his horse's leg.

He pulled, as a shriek sounded, and I thought it was my own.

But it was Cooper's horse that lashed out.

Kicked his skull with a loud *crack!*

Blood bloomed from his hair, through his eyes, to his grin.

And James Cooper of the town brigade fell forward.

Dashed and dead.

12

A dead man. A dead man. A dead man.

The river laughed low, as bleeding so full of fright, Cooper's horse bolted down the path, away into the woods.

A dead man. A dead man. A dead man.

Dead he was, there was no doubt. His skull was crushed. His hair clogged with blood, that soaked the stones beneath his body.

A dead man. A dead man. A dead man.

'Can you stand?'

I felt strong hands lift me gentle. That lady and I looked to each other, she a half-head taller than I, older by a year or two. Her cheek was all pinked and dirty. We breathed hard, hearts in our throats.

'You are hurt.'

The cut from Cooper's sword spilled red across my palm.

She shook a sash from her neck, white as a swan. She wound it about my hand. Her fingers were like drops of ice. Yet quick and careful she tied off that sash.

'There.'

She had a way.

'Here, help me.'

Cooper lay before us, his body twisted to question.

She kneeled, then she looked up to me, watching her, like I would always ever want to watch her. Her brow raised, and there crept a smile so very slight.

'We can get him off the path, if we roll him.'

I moved beside her, and like her took hold of his dead shape.

'With me,' she whispered, for it was our secret forever.

Then she pushed, and with her I heaved, and slowly, slowly we rolled Cooper like a log for winter. His face turned to the sky, eyes open, smiling still.

'Again.'

And with this woman of the woods, I pushed and heaved, so that Cooper rolled towards the drop. The trees rose from the sheer bank, and the sun spied yellow and green through the sighing leaves. It was as if they watched us in our work, rolling a dead man towards a river that called so brightly for his bones.

To me. To me. To me.

'Once more,' Greeneye said, sweat upon her brow.

And once more we rolled him, saw his eyes pass and look towards the drop that beckoned, till he left our grip and the dead weight of him carried him over, rolling faster and faster between the trees, through the sunlight, to the river who cried out as he plunged into her arms.

We stood, that lady and I, breathing, listening, thinking.

'His horse threw him,' she said. 'For this path is too dangerous, would you not say?' She plucked Cooper's last words from the air and tossed them after his body. How strange she was. This sprite who had saved me, fought for me and now seemed happy to bury a wicked wolf.

'Yes.' I nodded. 'Much too dangerous, my lady.'

She smiled again beneath that shifting light. In the blink of the sun, in the rustle of the leaves, we had planted something that grew there upon the bank of a hidden river.

'Are you hungry?'

Her green eyes turned to me as though they could see my empty belly.

I nodded again.

She wiped mud from her cheek. 'Then come.'

The lady moved to her horse. In a flurry of cloak, she was high upon him and reaching an arm to me. I took it without a thought and was pulled up fast. Her arm curled about me.

The horse turned without a sound, rocking beneath us, to clip and clop deeper to the dark of those woods. I shivered to be there, and for what had passed so sudden. Yet I felt good, safe.

'He spoke of...' my voice came quiet, I turned my head to feel her watching me, 'Whitaker Hall. Your home?'

'My father's estate,' she murmured, sounding sad. 'It is not far.'

A click of tongue, a flick of ears. We were so high upon that beast. I felt giddy. I had never ridden a horse. Dill had, many times.

'He came with news of your mother, no doubt,' the lady said soft. 'I am sorry...'

I did not speak, as tears would surely fall, and I did not want to cry before her. The horse stumbled. I gasped, yet she held me tighter.

'You are safe.' The path reached the bottom, became a track through the trees. 'And my Coal would never drop you.' She pressed her graceful fingers to his wide neck.

'I am not used to horses. Dill... my sister... likes them.'

I looked along the curving track. There was a shape becoming larger, big and brown among the leaves.

'Dill... That's a pretty name,' said the lady. 'Is she younger or older, your sister?'

'Younger.' The shape was a house. 'She is nine year...'

Sunlight found it then, sitting there among the trees. It was so grand, so many windows.

'And Dill rides?'

As Lady Greeneye coaxed her horse to slow, I thought of Dill shrieking with delight. Running and flinging her clothes away, her bare behind, a little moon.

'She has, many times.' Memory moved in me, like a hand dipped to cool water. 'One time she rode a farmer's carthorse, huge great feet, it had.' And I felt a chuckle coming quick, as that hand stirred deeper. 'She rode it one starry night, all naked she was. And she...' I laughed, and tears came sudden, like they had waited to pounce. 'She stood upon one leg as she rode.' The lady laughed with me and I felt her goodness flow from her body to mine. 'She was so funny... that night.'

The horse stopped, where the path led to a gate set to a wall of sandstone.

'I would like to meet this Dill of yours one day.' She dropped to the ground, then reached to me. 'I wager she could teach me a few things.'

As I came to ground, I stopped my laugh. This was the same Dill who most likely hated me for leaving her. I wiped my eye. The hand shook away the drops of my memory. I turned instead to see the gate in the wall showed a great garden beyond.

I felt the lady's cold hand upon mine. 'I am Anne,' she said, leading me to the gate. 'What is your name?'

Those green eyes looked deep to me like she knew me of old. Like she had been waiting for me upon that path in the woods, upon her horse dark as night.

'Eveline, but most call me Evey, which I like more.'

Anne put her hand upon the gate.

'Then welcome, Evey.' She smiled and pushed it open. 'Welcome to Whitaker Hall.'

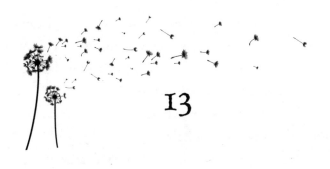

13

'Come,' Anne whispered, as though the garden slumbered, and she did not want to wake it. 'This way.'

And this way we went. The sun had clambered from her bed, and as a queen to her court, she smiled upon that grand place. Small stones cracked beneath our feet as we walked between beds of flowers. Some names I knew from Mother. Peaseblossom. Peony. Daffodil. But most I did not. When I stopped listening to her, I stopped knowing their names.

I breathed their scent rising in the warm. 'My mother… loved flowers.'

Two sparrows squabbled through rose bushes, bursting to bud.

'As did my sister.' Anne stroked a petal.

'Younger or older?'

She stopped. 'Younger, but she—'

The sound of feet turning on the stones, and from a path hidden by the bushes, there came a man. He was dressed in fine clothes, leather breeches and a feathered hat, which he lifted and swung low.

'Lady Anne, at last! I've been hunting for you.' He smiled, flicking his long hair.

'Sir Robert.' Anne took my arm. 'My father said… you were away at battle.'

'I was, my lady.' The fine man put back his fine hat. 'But after battle a man requires some rest and…' His whiskers twitched as he grinned. I felt Anne tense. '…Recuperation.' He played out his words, his gaze sliding to me.

'Who is this now?'

Anne drew me closer. 'A traveller… who has fallen on the road.'

I felt this man's eyes upon my dusty dress, my bloody hand, my dirty feet.

'She looks to me a waif, my lady.'

'She is a woman,' Anne's voice was hot, 'in need of help. And I mean to help her.'

The man called Sir Robert plucked a rosebud. 'Did you meet anyone else on the road?'

His question sent ice down my back, though the sun shone warm upon it.

Yet Anne did not waver. 'Meet anyone? Where?'

He peeled back the petals. 'The servants reported a horse with no rider passed by, not long ago.'

Cooper's horse. I swallowed to watch the petals fall from his ringed fingers.

'I don't know about that, my lord.' Anne looked him straight. 'I found only this poor woman. Now, if you please.'

'Lord Whitaker would not want a raggedy girl about his land.' He dropped the red bud, pressed it beneath his boot. 'Besides, I was hoping to spend some time with you. Alone.'

I watched a flush rise on Anne's neck.

'I am not my sister, Sir Robert.' Anne's green eyes glared.

'Indeed you are not, my lady,' his tongue darted. 'But your father will charge me to see off this...' He looked to me like he might a rat in the roses. 'And if it will bring us closer together, Lady Anne,' he doffed his hat, 'I will be only too glad to do so.'

'Do as you must!' She turned to me. 'Come, Evey, I will dress that wound.' And she pushed past his smile, rose thorns after catching her cloak.

'Who is that man?' I felt his following gaze.

Anne pulled me along. 'Sir Robert Danvers, a fool lord who plays my father, a greater fool for trusting him. My sister...'

I sensed Anne was to say more as Sir Robert still watched us, as a hound to its mark.

'Come, now. We do not have much time.'

We moved through those rose bushes, like a troop of red guards, to an open space before the house. I stopped in wonder. Those windows, like eyes looking to me. Ahead a door of oak arched above our heads. And then I felt something again, that hand stirring the pool of my memories.

I remembered Mother and I had once come to a noble place for a healing. And I remembered an arched door such as this. A woman lying still, white as her fine sheets. A man kneeling, silent with grief. A little girl, watching. And a baby's cry, over and on. I remembered Mother's words, breathing to my ear.

I cannot save her, Evey.

'This way, Evey.' Anne pulled me from my thoughts, on through those doors to a hall within. My skin prickled at the cool darkness, as that memory ebbed, leaving only shadows and closed doors.

But her daughters are strong.

I turned, feeling Mother's whisper to my ear, and as I blinked from day to dark, a girl stepped from the shadows, staring to me. Her pale, thin face floated in the gloom. She was dressed in stiff clothes. How was she here?

'Dill?'

I was shocked and pleased and shamed all at once. I needed to speak to her, to tell her. That what I did was for the best, that truly it was.

'Dill, I am…'

Anne clasped my reaching hand. 'Evey, this is Sarah.'

I blinked again and I saw a sad girl dropping her eyes to curtsey. She looked of Dill's age, for sure, nine year or thereabouts.

Dill was not there, for I had left her far behind, even as she begged me not to.

'We have a hungry guest, Sarah. Bring anything hot from the kitchen, some bread and ale.'

The girl who was not Dill looked back to me. I was no lady like her mistress.

'And a bowl of hot water.'

Sad Sarah nodded and went, and took away that dream of Dill, led her by the hand down the hall, till both were gone.

So with Anne I climbed a wide staircase, along a corridor lined with paintings, where sunlight from a window cast a path for our steps. There was a smell of dust, old wood mixed with the sweet air from the garden.

I thought I heard a sigh. The sun drew a yellow finger across a painting that made me stop and stare.

It framed a handsome woman looking straight and steady. She was tall, white skinned, with dark hair coiled beneath a hood. And I thought of Mother in her cowl turning from the hearth. The woman had a smile lifting slight, and bright green eyes that I knew well.

'My mother.'

Anne stroked the frame. I looked at that woman's watching face, her curving neck like her daughter's, their long arms, and long fingers... I started. Her hand rested upon a round, black stone. A Wolf Tree stone. Like Mother's. Like the one in my bag.

They have the witching way.

This house. The dying woman. The crying girl. I had been here. I knew I had. With Mother all those years ago. And here I was again. As if Anne had ridden out this day to find me. How could this be? And this woman. Her mother, a witch, to be sure. A fine, noble-born witch.

'I like to think she's watching over me.' Anne opened a door beside the painting.

I looked one last to that proud woman, her hand upon her scrying stone.

'I knows it.' I almost laughed aloud.

As her daughter closed the door behind me, leaving the witch of Whitaker Hall smiling in the sun.

14

Wood creaked beneath my feet, like I stepped out upon a still pond. And floating upon it, I saw a bed of cotton sheets with a quilt of many threads. A table and chair, a silver brush waiting for hair. And an oval mirror above them all, filled with the light that fell from a gilded window.

'Sit, Evey, please,' said Anne and so I did, upon that bed, smoothing that quilt under my fingers. I had not felt something so soft. I thought of the bed I shared with chatting Dill, and Mother coughing in the corner.

'Now, let us see...'

Anne whispered to wake the clothes in her closet and drew a pair of gowns. As she coaxed them to the air, I saw sadness hold her, yet she nodded, settling on one.

She laid it before me. The dress shone like everything in that room.

'I am not your size, I think.' I felt along the woven hem. It was scarlet, with tiny beads woven all about. It was as though I stroked the skin of a beautiful dragon.

'It was my sister's.'

Anne shook slight, then took my hand and unwound her sash, heavy with my blood.

A knock.

Sad Sarah carried a tray of meat, bread, apples, a jug of ale. My belly started.

'Is there water, Sarah?'

Anne turned my palm to the light.

'Y-yes, my lady,' Sarah stuttered. 'Hot, like you asked.'

As she placed the tray upon the table, she looked upon us, the dragon dress, my wound from a dead man's sword, her mistress tending my dirty claw.

'Thank you, Sarah.' Anne bent to my hand. 'That will be all.'

I smelled firewood and flour as the girl passed, and turned the door slow behind her, flicking those cow eyes to me.

Anne laughed. 'My, what a stir you cause in this house, Evey.'

She wrung the sash and my blood trickled pink in the light.

'I am not from your world,' I said, watching her wash my wound.

'This is true.' She nodded. The water smarted. I bit my lip as she pressed.

'But I would like to know more of yours.'

I watched her face moving in that bloody water.

'You have a healing touch.' I gobbled the meat and bread. 'Like my mother and my... sister.' Bread stuck. I choked.

Anne brought the flagon, and as I swilled the pain that clogged my throat, I thought on Dill. What if she had been harmed by Cooper? Or that horse had kicked her, not him? Had I not looked to her by leaving her? I chewed on my thoughts but tasted nothing.

'And you?' She smiled her curling smile. 'Do you have any gifts?'

How she looked to draw me in, as she drew out my pain.

'No... I am not like them.'

A bird chirruped beyond the window. A sparrow, bristling with cheek.

'Yes, I see that you are your own person, Evey.'

I looked to my wound as she daubed it over, feeling the slice of Cooper's sword.

'He will be found in time. That man on the road...'

'Yes.' Anne wrung blood to the water, blood over Cooper's face. 'In time, he will.'

There was no fear in her, this green lady of the woods.

I thought of us rolling him to the river. How good it felt. To do that with her.

'Why are you helping me, Anne Greeneye?'

She stood, and went whispering back to her closet, where she brought another sash fluttering to my cleaned palm. 'I had to, Evey.

'I saw that... man... coming for you. And I could not have it. I had to...' The sun shone through the cotton she tied off.

'He was going to kill you, Evey...'

She battled something. Did she have her own ghost? Like I had Mother, furious to me in her last.

'I knows it, Greeneye.' I looked over her healing handiwork. It seemed too clean to be my hand. 'But he was only after killing a witch. And witches are wicked, my lady. Did your mother never tell you that?'

I stepped to the window and looked down into the garden. My world did not shape trees, nor cut grass, nor plant roses like guards of honour. But Anne's mother? Wasn't she of this place?

They have a witching way.

As I looked, I saw an old man wrapped in a fur

cloak, moving with a cane and a limp. He trembled as he bent to the rosebuds.

'My mother told me...' Anne's voice ran like clear water. 'She always told me that a witch is a healer and a helper. A sage.' She moved behind me. 'From her, I learned that is your way, Evey.'

'No, I told you!' I turned to her. 'That is their way, not mine! I have no magick! I am not like them!'

The heat of my words held her.

'But then they came...' I breathed hard, as I turned from her gentle gaze, back to the window. 'Then everything changed.'

Anne stepped closer. I could sense her reaching to me.

'What will you do?'

'One dog is dead, Greeneye.' I looked to that garden, framed as a painting in the window. 'I have four to find before I am free...' I stopped myself. 'That is what I must do.'

The old man hobbled to another budding rose. His hand shook as he touched it, yet his face was still, lost to his thoughts. And in that moment, I knew him. A younger man trembling with grief for his wife, whiter than her sheet. As their new babe cried. And Death watched.

'She died from your sister's birth, didn't she?' I said. 'Your mother. She died from birthing her.'

Anne drew breath. The old man pricked his finger upon a thorn.

'How did...' Her voice fell. 'How did you know this?'

I watched as wind rushed through the garden and pushed a cloud across the sun and so my memory woke.

'I was here, Anne Greeneye.'

She stepped to my side.

'When?' She touched my arm. 'When were you here, Evey?'

'When I was a child. With Mother.' And I looked to her then and I saw the girl, so still with fear for that dying woman. 'Summoned to heal yours, no doubt.'

A sparrow landed upon the window ledge, eying us close.

'But we were too late.'

Anne's eyes grew wide and green as the garden. She stepped nearer, and I could smell almond soap upon her skin.

'I remember. The witch. Mother sent for her. Father would not have it, and I remember...' She reached to touch my hair. 'You!' And her young self stepped towards me then in that room of woe. 'You were the little girl at her skirts, with your hair so red...'

'Fat-cheeked and full of frowns.'

'Yes! It's you!' She startled the sparrow, and we watched it wing, up and round, across that window so fast that it seemed to plummet into the mirror we turned to, where two girls caught our gaze.

One was dark and tall, with eyes emerald bright, and a smile so gentle and sad. The other flame of hair, with a frown puckered upon her freckled brow, and a gap between her front teeth, which showed to smile.

Then together those girls laughed to see us, as we laughed with them and the sparrow sang his sweet song.

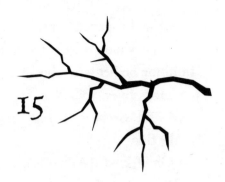

15

I had not laughed like that for so long. While Anne held sadness so close, that it seemed her laughter burst from her, like water from a dam.

'Come.' The elder girl stepped from the mirror, and I wanted to clutch her back, my new-found friend. 'You must make yourself ready.'

Her smile wilted as she helped me from my old Evey clothes.

'Is my time in your world ending, then, Anne Greeneye?'

I brought that dragon dress about my shoulders, felt its sigh of cotton lace.

Anne opened her mouth to speak, but no words came. She flushed, then turned to her closet, and drew out shoes and a cloak of such scarlet. Wool slid soft between my fingers.

'This was Jane's.'

'What happened to her?'

Anne shook her head, looking to the window, thinking on her father below.

'Here, Evey, your bag...'

As she swept it up, Mother's stone loosed and fell to the floor.

'Oh!' It circled Anne's feet as she bent to it. 'This is...'

'It's mine!' I blurted out, then I felt shame. She wasn't Dill, always fretful for it.

I watched her fingers trace over the black stone, turning it.

'Strange, I thought this was Mother's...'

That painting of her mother, her hand upon a scrying stone. A witch in this house of rose beds and gilded windows. A witch like Mother. Witches everywhere.

'When my mother died,' Anne moved to the window, 'my father blamed witchcraft, said she had dabbled, had been punished by God. And he cast everything she owned away.'

She watched her father in the garden below, holding the stone close to her chest, as if she nestled a bird waiting to fly.

'He was so angry, Evey, driven by grief. I pleaded with him, that I might have something of her. All I have is that painting. Nothing more.'

Her hands stroked the stone. I moved to her.

'This is all I have of Mother.' I took it from her gentle-like. 'Her scrying stone.'

Anne brushed the hair from my face, looking me over as though I was her sister, dressed for the day. 'And what is it you scry, Evey?'

Heat rose to my cheeks. 'I cannot.'

She raised an eyebrow, just like her watching mother, proud and powerful.

'I am not... I have no magick,' I said firm.

She laughed, 'Oh, but you are magick to me!'

I stared to her, and those tears glistening green and happy.

'I am?'

'Yes, you—' She stopped, hearing something beyond the window.

A voice below in that kept and cut garden. I turned to see Sir Robert hail his master. The old lord turned from his rosebud guard. We watched Sir Robert point to the window where we stood.

To us. To me.

Anne pulled me from their sight.

'We must hurry.' Worry tangled in her voice, her smile dying as she placed the food to my bag, then my old Evey dress, as those voices sounded on, yet I could not hear their words. Men murmuring. Bringing matters about.

'Your father would not want a witch in his house, I think.'

I swung into that scarlet cloak of her lost Jane, a smell of rose petals as it settled about me, its hood falling over my eyes. I felt bold, like a hawk watching from the shade.

I swirled to the window as might a fine lady. Anne's mother watched once from this window, like a dove cooped, yearning to fly.

The old man was too blind to see me. But that whiskered Sir Robert did right enough. When he saw me in Jane's scarlet hood, his brow furrowed. He looked as if he saw another. Looked with such fury.

A high scream rang out, shrill, full of pain. I threw my hands to my head.

'Evey? What's the matter?'

'Did you... I heard a cry, did you not?'

Anne had not screamed. But I was sure I heard it. I looked to the stone in my hand.

'It was a woman...'

I had looked to that furious man and felt a surge of many things. Anger and fear and something else, something deeper that stirred my body.

'It is only the horses in the stable.' Her hands pulled mine, fingers cold like pebbles from the river. 'And where you must go—'

'Wait. What happened to your Jane?' And still my heart beat over from that scream. I felt out of breath, as if I had been running.

Anne watched something at my shoulder that seemed to watch her back.

'Some months past, she…'

I pulled at Anne's fingers, urging those green eyes to tell their story.

'She was thrown by her horse.'

The men muttered louder still. Let them.

'She rode too fast that day into the woods.'

'I am sorry for it, Anne Greeneye.' But my voice sounded flat, not enough.

'My sister had such spirit, Evey,' She stroked the scarlet cloak about my shoulders. 'Jane wasn't like me. She was wilful and wild. She did what she wanted. You might as well stop the wind.'

How often I had said same for Dill. How different we were. Where Dill laughed, I frowned. As Mother let her run and play, so I worked my chores all day.

'And she was not like my father, who is deaf to my silly tales, who will not listen to me, who grieves for her just the same as me.'

'Jane was like my mother, you see –' she turned, gazed into the gloom, where her mother ever watched her sorrow – 'who loved her so.'

I reached to her. My Anne Greeneye, my lost friend.

'She loved you same,' I said, sure as the tears that marked her cheeks. 'Do not think that she didn't.'

The sparrow chittered from the garden. The muttering had stopped, and then a sound of feet, turning on stones.

'Damn them! Damn the men of this house!' She wiped her tears as her mind took hold of something. 'Damn that man who tried to hurt you! For Jane, I will do something!'

Her gaze burned green fire. There was such anger seamed deep within her. Like a poison that would not draw.

'Evey, listen to me. My father is the magistrate here. He signed the decree. There's going to be a trial.'

'A trial? For witches?'

'Yes. He is pressed by those around him. The puritan church. The militia. The will of the people. Their fear and suspicion. And he...'

She seemed to grow taller and minded me of that sprite I had first met in the wood, so strong and sure, so not to be passed.

'He blames my mother's death on witchcraft, like others blame this war against the king. His grief has changed him, Evey. And others use it, feed on it.'

'Others?'

'Those men. That came for you.' She smiled, full of sadness, anger and wile. 'I know where they will be.'

She took my hand again.

'At this trial they have staged. To cleanse their guilt with the blood of innocents. They will be there, Evey. In town. Not two days' ride. And a fine lady such as you, Evey, will need her horse, will she not?'

She smiled her wily smile to me.

'She will, my Lady Greeneye.' I smiled back. 'That she will.'

16

'That's it, Evey. Up you go.'

The saddle creaked, as I raised unsteady. Anne held the mare, who turned her bay head to watch me.

Through the stable door, I could see a cobbled yard, and beyond a muddied track. The sky was clear. Sunlight found the daffodils, and bluebells peeped to life.

'Be strong with her, for Shadow is wilful... aren't you, beauty?'

Anne stroked the horse's dipping nose, and its body twitched beneath me.

'She is... she was... Jane's horse.'

She was thinking on that day, when her sister rode wild into the woods, her scarlet gown flying in the wind.

'Be careful, Evey.'

Anne touched my hand bound by her sash. Birds called from the yard.

I looked down to her. 'I am… will ever be grateful for your help, Anne Greeneye.'

She nodded. She was going against her father. Fine ladies did not act this way.

'Jane must be free…' Her voice caught. 'Take her from this house.'

'Anne…'

'Shadow knows the way. Kick your heels. Quick now!'

Her green eyes burned me, as if she kicked me with her own heels and so I dug mine sharp and felt my stomach jolt as the mare surged from the stable.

'Good fortune to you, Evey! Always!'

The horse grew apace, I turned to wave.

'Stop!'

Running across the courtyard, brow like thunder, came Sir Robert.

'Stop, you damn thief!'

'She's not a thief! I gave her the horse!'

I pulled at the reins, but the mare hungered for freedom, and she bit down, moving all the faster.

'Ride, Evey!'

She snorted as she leaped across the yard, where Sir Robert pointed, furious, and Anne held him to see us go. Greeneye. My fiery friend who battled without knowing me, but who I knew all this time, a girl watching from the shadow, a lady waiting in the woods.

Take her from this house.

'I will, Anne Greeneye. I will free your sister...'

Trees rushed by, and the wind made me gasp, and I pressed my knees, feeling the warmth, the power, the joy of that horse called Shadow as she carried me on and away.

Soon the track turned beside a lake, silver in its stillness. On the far side stood a line of trees, like subjects along the way, where a heron, that silent king, watched the water.

I saw us there, a fine lady upon her high steed. I saw her cloak flowing, her dragon dress beaded and beautiful. I saw her looking at me from her hood, her hands gripping the reins, her bag slung about her.

The stone! I had left it upon Anne's floor, still rolling at her feet. I had left it.

No!

I drove my hand deep to the bag. And my heart started to find it, waiting for my touch. I closed my hand to its cool hardness.

And as I looked at the lady in lake, that silver stillness shifted and bent, and strange upon strange, another horse came beside her, and another, and another. Three men, turning as a pack. One was young and callow. Another heavy and bearded. And the last…

Tall One.

Holding something gagged and bound, a girl with black hair and white face, kicking and kicking.

'Dill?'

A splash. The heron flapped away with a fish.

The water rippled, but only that lady moved to watch me.

I shuddered as I smoothed the stone, feeling the many lines across it, like little wrinkles. Mother's face. What I saw, was that a vision? I had never had a gift for such things.

'For I am not you, Mother. Nor you, sister.'

That girl all bound. She looked so like Dill.

Shadow nodded beside her fellow in the water. And as we passed on, it was Grey's words that rose from the ripples.

When Dill struck Tally, it woke at the taste of her.

I looked again at the stone. What was it saying?

It is hungry, Evey.

Cooper was dead. That was right. Only three riders I saw. But that girl could not be Dill, while she was safe at the coven. My guilt was pricking me, playing tricks on my mind.

The heron rose above the trees.

Feed it the blood of your enemies.

And like those birds, ever my friends, leading me on, I came to it.

'See, Dill?' I laughed aloud. 'It ain't just you!'

I had seen those I would hunt, and those I would keep safe. Those like that ungrateful mite, ever telling me what she could do. Me and me alone.

We made the trees, our waiting subjects, and Shadow's hooves sounded upon the hard ground. And like a sword upon the wheel, Grey's words turned.

Give the stone all your anger, and it will make you strong.

'But scrying is so strange, my beauty.' I stroked Shadow's neck. 'Magick I may not have much, but I can fight and I can hunt, and anger I have... Anger I have aplenty.'

There, stretching long as a snake asleep in the sun, was the road to town.

17

We rode till the sun had smiled her most, and the shadows of the trees stretched down that dusty road. The only sounds were the mare's hooves ringing out, the draw of her breath beneath the rattling bridle, and the creak of the saddle where I moved.

'Did you throw your mistress?' I stroked her neck. 'Are you a killer, dear Shadow?'

She flicked an eye to me, yet I saw no spite in it. Anne said that Jane had been thrown that day by this horse. But there was something else to her story.

What had happened in that house of sadness? The mare's rough coat was warm beneath my hand. I clicked my tongue, as Dill had once shown me, and Shadow's ears twitched. Then they pricked forward, hearing something ahead.

I pulled her to halt, the reins biting to my fingers.

I heard a laugh. Another joined it. Children. But I could not see them.

'Come, Shadow, let us see what we can see.'

The mare sprang to gallop and I gasped as we made a bend.

A great train of people.

Gold clouds of dust rose about them. Men held to swaying horses where women sat, some with babes, some too old to walk. Children ran, happy pups yapping and hollering. A little girl pushed at a boy, who chased her. She laughed over her shoulder, until she turned and saw me beneath the tree. She stopped, her laughter swallowed.

The boy caught her, but she pointed to me. He shouted loud and quick, as he was taught to when he saw a stranger upon the road. And like the flame that sparks from tinder, word spread till that train of people stopped.

'Well met, there!'

Well met. Last time I heard those words, I fought a wolf on the road. Yet this train had women and children, with faces afeared of me. I would not have that.

'Well met!' I called back to put a murmur through their stillness. I was no wolf.

Shadow whickered to greet her kin, as we trotted near. They were a sorry band. The men drew their wives closer, while their babes looked on, dirty fingers to dirty cheeks.

'Lady!'

A mite, all dark locks and smiles, pointed to me, her great discovery.

'Lady, Mummy! Look!'

The mother drew her deeper into her shawl.

'I'm sorry for her, my lady,' said a young man, fair of hair, thin to the bone. 'She is only now after talking, and she has never seen a noblewoman.'

I had forgotten that I wore all that Anne had given, the dress, the cloak, the shoes.

Those people saw not me, but a fine lady, riding her fine steed. And then I saw it true. Anne wanted to free her sister from their house. So I would do it, I would be her Lady Jane of the Scarlet Cloak. Free and living in me.

'Good day to you all.'

Jane's voice was like Anne's. She bent her head to those watching faces and smiled from the shade of her hood.

The men touched forelocks, and the women dropped their gaze, but the children stared as children do. Lady Jane was a show worth watching.

'Pray, where do you venture?' I smiled at my words, flowing easy and true. I liked this Jane who could speak so soft and clear. 'You look troubled and tired, good people.'

The babe whined, pulling for milk.

The fair man looked to an elder with arms as frail as the stick he held to. He pointed a bony finger down the road behind.

'We seek the mercy of Lord Whitaker. Our children are hungry. Our village has suffered much in the fighting. Our crops failed, and there was no harvest... there was nothing... those parliament soldiers took it all.'

Fair Hair whispered to soothe his shaking head.

'And this morning more came, they took my Tess... took other girls...'

Cold stabbed my gut.

'Who? Who came?'

'They took my Beth!' a woman shouted, her face a furrow of tears. 'And her brother, my little Bob! But they done nothing!'

That cold turned to ice.

'Who took them? Tell me!'

My words sounded about that dusty road, then echoed with a cry. But it was not my voice, nor the cries of a child. It was a rider, behind me.

Fast, galloping through the shadows. The crowd swayed, as fear swept among them.

The little girl I had first seen clutched to Fair Hair. 'Is it him, Daddy? That tall man who took Beth?'

And my heart held.

'Who did you say?'

'Stay back there!' Fair Hair shouted. 'Whoever you are! We have suffered enough!'

Jane had no blade. Only a stone that I barely knew how to use. I reached into my bag.

'Declare yourself, stranger!'

I weighed the stone in my hand. I knew how to throw.

A cry, and a wave. It was a woman, upon a steed black as... coal.

Anne.

My heart leaped. I thought I would never see her again. Yet she raced towards me, and as she drew nearer, I could see her smile wide with the wind. My Greeneye was come to me.

'Be not afeared.' I turned to the frightened folk. 'She is my friend. She is my friend!'

Then Anne was upon us, bringing Coal snorting to a halt. A green cloak fell long about her. A bag was slung and strapped. She was set to journey.

'Lady Jane...' Anne's cheeks were pinched red. 'I have found you!' She gasped from her ride, from finding me, and I wanted to fling my arms about her.

'Two ladies!' The little girl pointed a wet finger.

'Why, yes. What a clever thing you are.' Anne reached and tickled the girl, who blushed and hid to her mother. Anne looked to the wary men, the tired women, to Fair Hair, and Old Father.

'Well met.'

They only nodded, some touching forelock, but all were struck still by this woman upon her dark steed. I knew that feeling.

'Lady Anne,' I said. 'These people are suffering. They seek shelter from your father.'

Then murmuring they crowded close, all fear gone. The old man leaned upon the arm of Fair Hair. Anne watched them, shock and sorrow fixing her smile.

'What has happened here?'

'Witch hunters, your ladyship!' cried Old Father. 'They came to my sisters when it suited them, didn't they? When they wanted scrying? When they wanted charms and spells aplenty. When they wanted to win their bloody war!'

'Father, shush, now. He does not mean this, they were just old women.'

'No, lad!' He pushed at his son. 'They were witches, and everyone knew it, for everyone came to them. Young and old, rich and poor. Even Lord Whitaker himself!'

He raised that bony finger to Anne. She knew too well.

'Wise women, scryers, healers! Whatever names we have for them, they had the witching way. And those men… so quick to counsel them for their warring, the quicker they were to take them and hide their plotting. A war won by magick? That could not be. That would not be!'

The woman gripped to Anne's saddle, fresh tears running.

'But why my Bethy? Why my Bob? Why them? Tell me why?'

I swallowed to watch them. Anger curled my hands to fists.

Anne shook her head. 'I'm sorry, I do not know.'

Old Father struck his stick on the road.

'I told you, Mary! For Beth is flame-haired. They sought a young witch with red hair. A warrior witch they called her.'

My fists shook. They sought me. Yet took another.

Anne looked quick to my hood that hid my hair. My dangerous hair.

'Where is your village?' she said, quiet fury simmering.

Fair Hair stepped from his trembling father. 'On this road to town, my lady, but you should not stop there.'

'Yes, they should, boy! These noblewomen should stop. See what has become of this land! What has become of us all!'

And he began to cough and weep and hold to the woman Mary.

'Lord Whitaker will give you shelter and food.' Anne pulled Coal to pass them, and so drew the mare. 'Tell him his daughter, Lady Anne, sent you... Ha! Coal!'

That fire burned brighter and bolder in her, and I would follow its flame. And I knew Fair Hair, Mary, Old Father, they each felt its heat as we passed on into that fading light.

'Tell my damn father that, you hear me!'

18

Old Father's words beat in my mind, as the horses' hooves drummed the road.

They sought a young witch with red hair. A warrior witch they called her.

A girl had been taken. But it should have been me.

'Evey, look...'

Smoke in the sky, like the tail of a creature, curling lusty to the air.

'The village is close, Anne...'

'Then faster!'

Her horse raced away, dust flying from his loud heels. I urged Shadow in their wake, and we galloped towards that smoke, a dread welcome, beckoning.

We were on a muddy track from the road that led through fields, when we saw two plough horses. There was no driver to guide them, so they stood, watching the birds peck and hop.

'Evey, why do they…?'

But Anne's question held. Its answer lay ahead, as the track found a huddle of houses.

We urged our skittish steeds into smoke and stillness.

They were low houses as my own home had been. A room with a hearth and beds for a family. And like my own, they were empty. Each door splintered, where a musket and a boot had kicked it open and strewn what lay within. Broken bowls, bits of food, torn clothes. Things of no worth to a militia man, but everything to the folk who lived there. Then we saw the dead.

A man face down, stretched across a threshold, as if he crawled to leave, but was stuck in his blood pooling upon his step.

Outside, a woman sat staring, shocked by the hole in her heart.

A chicken scratched seed from a sack, its dry guts slashed to the ground.

'Oh, my…'

Anne stepped to another home. At her touch, a shutter groaned its last and fell away. Four more houses cowered about a trough tumbled to vomit water and straw. Nothing moved but the smoke. Tall

One's pack had put the torch to all that they had found. Or didn't find.

'All this…' Anne coughed. 'For witches.'

'Aye.' My laugh was bitter. 'Minds me of home, Greeneye.'

I tied Shadow, and she nosed through the leaking trough, when a goat stepped from a doorway, chewing a stolen crust. It bleated, then fled, bounding through the smoke beyond the turn of the house.

Yet still it cried, so strange, not like an animal, more like—

'Evey!'

We ran to the sound. Fields stretched beyond the house, where a cart was turned upon its side, its wheels slowly turning. A broken chair. A row of shattered barrels. And the goat, chewing over the body of an old woman. But the body moved and cried,

'Help… Help me…'

We rushed to her, and Anne turned her gentle. A great weal was across her eye.

'Water…' she gasped.

I brought a scoop from that sorry trough. The old woman shook to drink.

'What is your name?' Anne stroked her matted hair.

'Ah…' Pain writhed through her. 'Tess, young 'un. Tess, I am.'

Anne looked to me. The old man's Tess.

'We met the others, your husband upon the road…'

'John!' She seized my hand, tears running. 'Is he safe? Did they get away?'

I swallowed my ache as I watched her, for I was minded so strong of Mother, when they came and broke our lives apart like these blasted houses. The goat began to bleat.

'Yes, Mother.' I could not help her name escape me. 'Your John is safe.'

Tess sighed, closing her eyes. Did she see him?

'What happened?' Anne said. 'Your husband told us you were taken…'

Her eye flickered. 'They had us both right enough, Jess and me… my sister…' She coughed. 'But I brought that chair across the back of one… he didn't see me in the smoke.' She chuckled, blood upon her old teeth. 'I got him good.'

She moaned as pain seized her, brought her hands to her belly.

'But another stuck me, and they took Jess… They took her from me, my twin, my sister dear.'

Anne moved to Tess's belly. The old woman shrieked.

'She has a deep wound, Evey…'

Blood on Anne's fingers.

'They betrayed us!' Tess shuddered. 'That Witchfinder... so keen he was for our help! And help him we did, if he swore to let us live free!'

Blood on her fists.

'But he lied. For he is scared...' Her eye grew wide as she gripped my arm. 'He even has a child, a scrap he has taken along the way. Oh, he is a monster! A lying, scared fiend!'

'Here now.' Anne brought water to her white lips. 'Evey, we must get her back to John, help me.'

But Tess pushed her away. 'No! No! Leave me! I am dying!'

Anne shook me. 'Evey, please...'

As I looked at my friend, full of worry, I thought of Mother, how she shouted at me to go. How in her last, we had fought.

'Evey, listen to me, we must help her!'

And I remembered Mother's eyes, black with fire, as she screamed.

For my blood...

Anne shook me.

Your blood...

Your sister's blood.

So much blood.

'Evey!'

And Mother rolled, dead in the mud. And I left her.

'Evey! Wake up!'

A smack across my cheek. I felt it.

'Evey, you were... I don't... I am sorry I hit you, I need your help. I'm sorry.'

I watched Anne as she rocked Tess like a babe, small and still.

'I'm sorry.'

As she stroked her, as she closed her old eyes.

'I'm sorry.'

19

As dusk drew down, we found what we could about that village, to bury the dead.

With a broken shovel and a blunted axe, we dug and we dug, till the hole was deep and done. Like close cousins, we shouldered up the old woman, and brought her along with whispers to the grave. The staring girl, we laid gentle to the bed where she sat. We did not have strength to free the fallen man from his door. Husband and wife, brother and sister, or fair neighbours two, we did not know. Only that the foxes would come soon enough.

I watched Anne pull buttercups and strew them upon faces that did not flinch. As cold came across the fields, we tucked the dead beneath blankets of dirt. They were good and buried and gone.

Wind stroked my cheek, and I felt that smack of Anne's palm. I knew I had frozen, watching Tess, but seeing Mother. What they did to her.

'It is done,' Anne sighed. 'We must rest, Evey.'

I looked to the grave, to the blasted homes. They were like skulls, stripped of flesh. Broken windows for staring eyes, doorways like open mouths.

'Aye, but not here.'

The fields stretched empty, back along the track to the road.

'There, Evey!'

Beyond those horses stuck waiting in their plough was a barn. It hunkered beneath an oak tree, that stood alone, an old king in a deserted realm.

'Come on.'

We brought our steeds and made across the field towards the two horses.

'Wait...'

Anne alighted and freed the pin to their plough. But those horses only watched us ride on through the drifting smoke and falling shadows. In my mind I saw them still, and ever will, waiting for a master who would never come.

The old barn was empty and smelled dry, a door hanging half-open. Shaking the ache from our bodies, we crept in, quiet as the mice that hid there.

There was a ladder raised to a stage above, a pile of

old sacks for a bed. It was laid on right proper. Sleep gnawed my bones.

'Help me, Evey.'

Anne brought a blanket from Coal's saddle, and I hefted her bag, heavy with things.

'We will eat tonight at least.'

And so upon that blanket near the open door, she placed bread and cheese, some nuts, a fist of ham and a flagon of ale. How like children at a winter's feast we fell to that food in hungry silence, tearing and sharing, and ate till we could eat no more.

'Ah, I will burst.'

Anne took up a bag of oats for the horses, feeding them each, stroking them as I watched their shadows. A song played across my tongue, and I hummed to the closing day, to the sleep that beckoned, to what lay ahead tomorrow. Town. Meakin. Caldwell. Tall One. Tall One. Tall One.

'What is that melody?'

Drawing her cloak about her, Anne sat close, her shoulder to mine. The song had come running to me with little feet I knew so well.

'It is from a song that Mother used to sing. To my sister, to get her to sleep. Or if she was hurting.'

I drank from the flagon, feeling the ale flow warm. I swigged again.

'Sing it for me.' Anne took the flagon. 'I would like to hear your mother's song.'

I swallowed the sweet ale to swill the ache that brewed there.

'Please, Evey.'

She stroked my arm as we watched the day breathe its last. So I gathered, and I sang to the fields drawn to dusk, and our horses grazing to rest. I sang to Greeneye as she rested her head to my shoulder.

'Dilly Doe, my Dilly Dee,
Dilly Dancer of the Day.
Dilly of the moon, Dilly of the stars,
Dilly of the dawn that I see,
Dilly Dee, Dilly Dear,
Dilly Doe, Dilly Do.
Oh, my Dilly Dancer of the—'

My throat felt like a hand had closed it. I swung again at the ale, but I could not swallow and I choked it out.

'I am... sorry. I cannot...'

Anne's fingers crept to mine.

'Don't be,' she said. 'Evey, what is the matter?'

For a moment, I did not understand her, till I felt the tears trickle upon my cheeks. I wiped them away, but they only ran the faster.

'It is the ale.' I tried to laugh.

'It is your mother's song,' Anne said so gentle. 'Back at the village, with the woman, Tess… you were thinking of your mother, weren't you?'

And my tears made me mute.

'Evey, Evey, you are grieving, and you must let it come.'

And I looked to her green eyes then. Full of thoughts of me. If only she knew.

'You mourn your mother. You miss your little sister. Of course you do.'

'I left them! I left them all!'

My voice cracked, wrung from deep in my chest.

'That day the men came hunting for us,' I gasped as if I was running again, 'I had argued so with Mother…' Tears caught my breath. 'I told her…'

Anne nodded, drawing it from me.

'I told Mother I didn't want her stupid witching way no more.'

And I was there, remembering, shouting at her.

'Told her she could be happy with… stupid Dill, her stupid favourite, after all!'

I felt the sting of my words as I hurled them at Mother's face.

'And she…' I remembered how I cried, how I wanted to hurt her. 'She told me to get away from her house! That I was a red monster! That, yes, Dill was her favourite if I was so wicked to them! She shouted at me to get from her sight, go now from this house! And so I did. I ran from her, hating her. Hating her so much!'

'Evey.'

But I was not all told. Anne would know how wicked I was.

'I was running from her, out to the road. I felt such anger and such joy, because I was free. To show her, to make my own way, you see?'

Anne nodded, smiling her sad smile.

'Then...' I could hear them now. The horses. The shouts of that pack.

'They came, and everything was so fast, and Dill and I watched them come and... hit Mother... and... and...'

My tears became a torrent, my chest heaved with such pain. Such terrible pain.

'Evey, there's nothing you could...'

'You don't understand!' I cried. 'We were so horrid to each other in our last, and then she gave her stone to Dill, not to me, her eldest!'

Anne's fingers wiped the tears from my chin.

'What's wrong with me?' I cried my rage across the field. 'All she could say was, "Swear you will ever look to Dill"!'

Anne stroked my wet cheek. I shook my head away.

'Evey, she wanted you safe is all. Those men—'

'Those men!' My voice shook through the shadows. 'Those men who killed her and now I will not be free till they are dead.'

Anne nodded. 'I know…'

'Then know that I have not left her at all. And I cannot leave home…'

Anne's green eyes so trusting. Would she be my friend still if I said it?

'Till they are all dead because,' I felt sick to say, but I would, I could not stop, 'because it's like Mother is alive still, watching me. And I cannot stand it. I have to be free of her, Greeneye.'

I laughed my wicked laugh. 'Mother was right, I am a monster!'

'Evey, you are not!'

I smiled at her as though she was a trusting child and I her murdering mother.

'I tricked my sister. You didn't know that, did you?'

Anne only watched me. Perhaps she should leave me, else be caught in my wickedness.

'I left her with people we barely knew. I tricked her and I took the stone. And I lied, I told her it was for the best.'

Pain surged afresh through me. I felt I would scream for its burning. It hurt so much that I felt laughter, but instead came a sob that rushed sudden from me.

'But that wasn't true, Greeneye! It wasn't true! I left her because I didn't want her. I didn't want her telling me ever and over how she liked this spell and that charm, how much she liked to learn magick. I didn't want her silly gifts and being good at healing and making Mother proud. I didn't want her stupid laughing and dancing. So… I took it, this… thing!'

I reached to my bag, and grabbed out the stone, Mother's shawl spilling, like she lay before me.

'I took it because I knew it would hurt her!' I waved the stone in the air. 'For I have no magick. I have no gift like her and I never will!'

Anne drew me to her, and I sobbed into her shoulders. It would not stop. It would not stop. And I did not want it to. I felt I would cry till the earth opened and took my sorry body down, away, and gone for good.

'And I was glad then, do you see now? I was glad to be rid of Dill, that I hurt her, that I had this… this… stone that I don't understand.'

And I looked at the stone that I held across Anne's back, as her fingers stroked my red monster hair.

'Because I hated her.'

'Hush, you did not, Evey.' She held me tighter.

'But I did so, my lady,' and I could not see the stone or Mother's shawl for tears. 'I hated her because she was so different from me. And now...'

Anne's fingers smoothed over and over my monster back. Guilt writhed in my gut.

'I miss her silly way. Everywhere I see her face!' I laughed and sobbed. 'Isn't that stupid? Tell me.'

'No, Evey, it is not.'

'I am a wicked sister, I'm a bad daughter...'

'No, Evey, you are not.'

'And Mother's dead...' My sobs grew and grew as Anne held me, yet I shivered on. 'And I'm scared. I'm so scared.'

'Shush, now, I know, Evey. I know...'

Then Anne rocked me as I cried for what I had done and could not mend, and the darkness came to find me.

20

Town. It lay before me, beneath a sky stained with smoke, where gulls wheeled and screamed. A great hungry thing, swallowing the crowds that milled towards its mouth. How strange. That all upon this long road, strove from the light of the land, to burrow into that belly, full of noise and dirt and woe. How I wanted to rear Shadow sudden and turn with Anne to scatter the herd with eyes only for that bleak place.

But those dogs lay hiding there. Tall One and his bloody brood. I could feel their beating hearts within the great stone body ahead. I could smell their stench among the hawkers' stalls that cluttered our path.

'Roast pigeon! Nice roast bird for the lady!'

I growled and waved the man aside. His meat turned my stomach. Like the hungry swell of buyers and sellers. I knew what this was, this drool for barter, this dream they shared. Trial Day was coming.

Trial Day meant witches. And witches were good for business.

'There will be guards, Evey.'

Anne strained to see above a rattling cart heaped high with boxes. She looked to me, her face all the whiter in the shadow of those walls.

'Are you ready?'

Beneath her sister's scarlet hood, I could only nod, for there was no turning back now. My own business with town was greater than this eager mob, whose mutters and worries weighed the air. I watched them flow forward. A boy slapped his lowing cow. A merchant dabbed dust from his cloths. A young family fussed their finery. A trial, such a treat.

'My cousin has a house within the walls,' Anne said. 'Once we pass through the gates, he will give us safe harbour for the night.'

'Keep moving!'

Shouts from ahead made the crowd stir.

'This way, I say!'

A soldier sat astride a piebald steed. A blade at his waist. He swung a boot at the cart, where an old man drove his old horse.

'Move along or we'll be here till nightfall!'

His voice was rough, his bald head burned by the sun.

'You heard the captain, wind it up, Father Time!'

With a piping laugh, a younger soldier, fair of hair, leaned to the open gate. He picked his nails with a knife, marking the flow of people as they passed.

Soldier men. Soldier men. My heart drummed.

'You there!'

Heads turned to us.

'To me, your ladyships, if you please!' The captain raised gloved fingers.

Anne leaned to whisper. 'Keep your hood up, talk little.'

'Fret not, sister,' I said as Jane, smooth and light. 'I will not shame you.'

She pressed my arm, as the captain's horse split the crowd, like the herd for the hound.

'Your ladyships, what brings you to my town on this fine evening?'

It did not feel fine. I wanted away from this big man with his prying eyes and his tittering cub. Yet something picked at my senses like that boy's blade upon his dirty nails.

'We visit my cousin, a wool merchant upon Sadler Street.' Anne tugged Coal from the piebald's sniffing. 'Is all well, Captain?'

He turned from Anne to the pushing people.

'Is all well? Now there lies a question, my lady.' His chest heaved as if a weight lay upon it. 'The king is routed. This town is parliament's now. So, aye, if that is well, then well it is.' His mind moved among the stomping crowd. He seemed tired, burdened. Then he shook awake and his gaze fell to me, under Jane's hood.

'Is your kinswoman too shy to come out today?'

The blond boy laughed. He looked me straight. I did not like this boy.

'My sister is tired from our journey, Captain…?'

'Meakin, your ladyship. John Meakin.'

In that show of teeth, I knew this name.

Meakin from town.

Given me by old Croake, who had lost all he loved.

'And why are you not travelling with an escort, my lady?' Meakin turned his soldier gaze over our horses, our clothes, over me.

One of Tall One's pack. Right before me. I felt Anne stiffen.

'Why, Captain, of course we were,' she lied so well. 'But as we reached the safety of the crowd, I turned them home.'

Meakin watched Anne, his soldier mind weighing her words.

'And where, your ladyships, is home?'

'Pray, now,' Anne cut in quick, 'who is your fine-looking fellow, Captain?'

His picking pup jumped at that.

'I am Tom Caldwell, my lady.' And he bowed his blond head, flashing his blade, and again I heard Croake's cry.

Tom, they called him. A wicked lad.

Meakin rolled his eyes. 'Here we go...'

'Soldier, journeyman, adventurer! At your service!'

Caldwell laughed his shrill laugh. Two of them. Two dogs before me.

Anne pressed her leg to mine. But from within Jane's hood, I could not stop it come.

'Adventures, you say, gentlemen?'

They started at my voice. *Yes, look to me. For I am sweet and I have a secret for you.*

'Have you had many, good sirs?'

'Why, yes!' Caldwell whirled his blade like he painted a picture. 'We caught the witches for the coming trial!' He lunged to stab the air.

'Witches!' Lady Jane put her shaking hand to my mouth. 'Were you not scared?'

'Evey...'

Meakin bent to my hood. *Closer, dog, and I'll give you a treat.*

'Not I, your ladyship!' swaggered Caldwell. 'Though one cast foul curses!'

In his gait, how he had stepped same to Mother. Sweat itched my lip.

'But all was well. I cracked her dead and gone!' He swung his fist at Mother's head. I thought to rip that blade from him and plunge it to his neck.

'But the captain here lost her witch daughter, a red-haired fox.' Caldwell raised his trusty blade. 'He swoons for her at these gates. Thinks she will come seeking revenge!'

'She will come, boy,' Meakin growled. 'Mark me.'

'Oh, revenge!' Jane licked her soft lips. 'How delicious, Captain!'

'Yet I think my captain fears her!'

'Enough, boy.'

Anne held my shaking arm, for I wanted them so, so much.

'Will you be at the trial, Captain?' she said. 'With brave Caldwell here?'

'Why, yes,' Meakin rumbled. 'It will need a guard…'

'Oh, we'll be there all right.' Caldwell showed his thumb, scabbed with blood. 'One of those little devils bit me! I will see her hang for it!'

'There are children at the trial?' How Anne drew him.

'Two devils,' Meakin spat. 'I only caught them. Orders is orders.'

Something in me snapped.

'Captain, is it true about the witches and the war?'

He turned that weary gaze to me.

'Is what true, my lady?'

'Hey! Move along there!' Caldwell ran towards a cart stuck in the mud.

'That your militia used witch magick to win your war.'

At that, Meakin's soldier eyes were tired no more. I would wake him.

'And is it true you seek to silence those who helped you? For surely a war won by witchcraft would turn the people…?'

'Where did you hear that?' Meakin came closer. Anne gripped me tighter.

And Evey, not Jane, smiled her vixen smile.

'Why, from a witch, of course.' I smiled as I shook. 'A dead and buried witch.'

'Get that rotten beast moving, you layabout!' Caldwell shouted to the sleepy driver.

'Who are you?' Meakin frowned, eyes darting.

'Why, Captain…'

'Evey, no!' Anne pulled me. But I shook free.

'I am what you have been waiting for…'

I threw back Jane's hood, so that his old soldier gaze took me all in.

'I am that red-haired fox…'

I laughed as he gaped.

'That witch daughter you wait on.'

He blinked, then went for his blade.

'Away, Coal!'

Anne kicked hard both horses. We leaped past Meakin's steed.

'Stop! Caldwell! Stop them!'

Caldwell turned, but that brave boy was too late. Anne lashed out. He fell to the mud.

'Whoa!'

And the old carthorse shied in fright, a wheel sheared with a crack.

'Stop, I say!'

'Out of the way!' Anne rushed the mob, towards the fallen cart and, 'Ha!' Coal leaped, high and over.

'Evey! Come on!'

I looked behind me. Meakin urged his steed to charge, Caldwell staggered to stand.

'After her!'

'Evey!'

I looked to Anne's white face, then to the cart. Could I jump it? This was Jane's horse, and she rode her like the wind, so I would. I must.

'Ha, Shadow!'

The mare sprang from my heels, and I gripped her with all my might.

'Stop!' Meakin bellowed. 'By my order!'

Shadow rose, and the cart slipped below me.

With a snort and a gasp we were down, and Anne was pulling me into the gates, the noise and the smoke.

But I saw the captain. And he saw me, as the crowd flowed about. How my heart fluttered.

'Your witch has come, John Meakin!'

He watched me, till he could see me no more, only hear my laughter.

'And she promises with all her heart, you shall meet her again!'

21

'Evey, that was foolhardy!'

Anne was not smiling like me, as we pushed on through those dusky streets.

The horses slowed with the milling of people. A window opened and with a cry, dirty water sluiced the cobbles.

'Those men were armed and—'

'Those men killed Mother! That means Tall One is here, so I must find a way to get to them, Greeneye. I must!'

Two men carrying a crate stopped to watch. I cared not.

'We will find a way, Evey, I promise. But we must be stealthy, or we will be lost. The captain's men will be looking for us now. My cousin's house is not far, come.'

She kicked on through the crowd. Far above, gulls cried in the reddening sky, and fast we made a crossroads. And there, on a nailed scroll, was daubed an old crone with leering eyes, a nose hooked, and talons that dangled a babe above a fire. Behind her lurked a baleful thing, tall and hairy, with horns and legs of a goat.

'*A Trial of Seven*,' Anne read the words that I could not, '*accused of Witchcraft, by order of the magistrate, his grace, Lord Whitak—*' she faltered. Her father.

Down those gloaming streets a bell began to toll.

'Is it an army? An attack?' I looked to the people rushing.

'No, Evey, it's the curfew bell. We must be off the streets.'

We reached a turning, where beacons were lit. I smelled oil from their smoke, as mothers called to children, and men bellowed at boys to batten down.

'This way.'

We spurred on, shutters all around banging and locking.

'We are close! Hurry now!'

It was as if those folk heeded her words, running like rabbits who smelled the fox, till only the sound of the bells remained. And us, two ladies, seeking shelter in the shadows of that frightened town.

Knock! Knock!

It sounded so loud in the empty street. Silence then, but for the breathing of our horses, the beat of our waiting hearts. At the street corner, a beacon flickered red in the gloom, two dogs battled for a bone.

I looked to the door knocker, a ram's head of silver with a ring in its mouth. It sat upon a courtyard door, and around its frame grew little leaves of stone. Cousin Peter was monied. A wool merchant, Anne said.

'Who's there?'

A man's voice. Firm. Not afraid.

'Peter.' Anne stepped closer. 'It is Anne. Your cousin, Anne.'

The starving dogs started. Many feet were coming. Marching.

Bolts shot from the door. The marching stopped.

'Halt! Who's about?'

The door scraped ajar and a lantern floated in the night air.

'Anne? What are you doing here?'

The man's face looked out. It was round and kindly. His thick hair was unkempt and flecked with grey.

'Who's about there? By my order!'

'Is your father taken ill?' said the merchant man.

'No, Peter, but… we need shelter. The night patrol…'

'Of course, of course! Come. Bring the horses through. Quickly now, quickly.'

He stepped from the light to unbolt the frame high above the door. It swept full open to the street, bringing a smell of dry hay and warm stone. A smell like home.

'Clear the street or face arrest!'

Soldiers. A beacon lit round helmets, staffs, muskets.

'Hurry with those horses!' Peter became a prancing shadow, inky spots on his fingers. 'Ah, just some late business, Captain, nothing but a little late business!'

He shoved Coal's rump, as we drew the horses into the courtyard. Peter pulled the door to.

'Take your business off the street!' came a stern voice. 'Do you not know curfew law? Are you wanting a night in the cells with the witches?' Anne reached for my hand.

'Ah, no,' came Peter's voice, 'that would not be my abode of choice. I am sorry for the trouble. Goodnight, Captain!'

'Then stay out of sight or you're witch meat, you hear? Patrol away!'

In the swinging lantern light, Peter put a spotted finger to his lips. We listened to the march of those boots, and the courtyard seemed to grow around us. Haybales, barrels, some boxes, a saddle. Another horse watched from the shadow, eyes gleaming. A cobbled floor beneath us had thick posts to the ceiling, and a door open to the house within, where more lights glowed like fireflies above an evening marsh.

'They are gone. Come into the warm,' said Peter.

A row of candles spluttered upon a long table that edged a hearth filling one wall, where a fire sat fat and happy. Pictures, trinkets were about walls of wood all aglow under the candles. In the far corner was a climb of stairs. And by the doorway where we stood, a desk slumbered beneath papers like fallen leaves, and a feather quill wept black tears for its master's hand. This was the home of a merchant man, right enough. It had things aplenty, floors above. I was minded of Anne's house. So many new places, so different and strange. Like this man was to me, yet I smelled no danger in his house, only wood, soot and the sweet smell of cooking. My belly growled and made Anne laugh.

'Peter, this is my friend, Eveline. She is the reason I—'

'Reasons after we quieten that gut, eh?' Peter closed the door and smiled. I caught his eye, quick and clever.

'Sit, sit, sit.'

So we did, as he brought cheese, a bowl of apples wrinkled yellow from their store.

'Eat! Eat! I insist! Now, Jessica baked some excellent bread...' He foraged the fireside.

I took some cheese, and chewed into its salty goodness, then looked about as I swallowed. Near the desk of paper leaves was another door to the street, and above it an old musket and blade pinned. Strange charms for a man of ink. The windows were shuttered tight, and I thought of the townspeople hidden in their homes as those soldiers scraped and booted about their sullen streets. Surely this curfew was a thing made of men.

Peter placed a flagon of wine, and a loaf that sang with smell. The bread broke warm and soft beneath my hands. Peter filled cups and we watched as he tossed back, wiping his mouth, that twitched to speak, till he could stand it no more.

'So, Anne. Tell me, what is this about?' He filled his cup again. 'Does your father know you are here?'

A squeak from the stairs. Did someone other listen for Anne's tale?

'No, cousin. I am not his dove to be coted and counted.'

'Then, you have run away?' He swilled and frowned. 'Don't you know how dangerous it is out there?'

'Peter, I am no child.' Anne put down her bread. 'Were you not younger than I when you "ran away" to sea? Leaving your nobility, your own cage, for a life of danger?'

Anne had flown hers, that we both could see, and how she grew into her wings.

Peter turned a ring upon his finger, as like he might test a key in a lock.

'And who is your hungry friend here?' He nipped again at his wine.

'I am Eveline.' I swallowed his bread.

'Eveline of…?'

He raised his cup and drank as I thought on this, and only one answer came to mind. Strange that it should be that name Mother had given me when I was a mite, that I had so squirmed from. But it was all I had, and it fit his asking.

'…of the Birds.'

Peter swallowed, and slow he wiped his mouth. In his eyes, I saw the sea moving.

'I heard many things in many lands.' He smiled and touched our cups, and it seemed we sat in his cabin upon the rising waves. 'But none as beautiful as that name.'

I felt heat come to my cheeks for sudden I felt proud.

'It is the name my mother gave me, Peter Merchantman.'

Peter laughed and slapped his leg. 'Peter Merchantman! Seems you've given me a name too, young Eveline. Ha! Peter Merchantman!'

As I watched Peter so merry, the stair squeaked again with our listener.

'Peter, Eveline is seeking someone, very urgently. And I mean to help her.' Anne looked to me. 'She believes they will be at the trial.'

Peter stopped his chuckling. 'The witch trial? Who do you seek there?'

'Tall One and his pack of dogs,' I said. 'Those that still breathe anyways.'

'Dogs? Is he a trader this… Tall One?'

In the shifting candlelight, he looked to my red hair, my rough hands. I was no lady, like his cousin who reached to him.

'Peter, Eveline has suffered so very much and—'

'I talk of those men who are dogs, for what they done.' My throat prickled as the words fought not to be told. 'They came to our home…'

And finally I drew them, from beneath their boots, from her bare body, still in the mud.

'They killed my mother.'

Peter stared to me, his cup to his mouth, his hair standing on end.

'Now tell me, Peter Merchantman with a blade

above your door.' The candles cowered to my whisper. 'Would you seek revenge, if they killed yours?'

'I would not rest from it.' His gaze held mine. 'And I am sorry that you cannot.'

Was our listener on the stair sorry too? I hoped so. I hoped the whole town was sorry.

'Would I know these men?' He filled our cups, filled his own.

The wine curled about my tongue. 'Would you know a witch trial without Tall One, without its Witchfinder?'

'The Witchfinder? Matthew Jacobs!' Peter's wine spilled like a wound opened. 'By all the saints!'

'Daddy! Daddy! Daddy!'

Down the stairs came running a little girl in her nightdress, curls gold in the light, cheeks rosy with sleep.

'Aunty Anne!' And she leaped to Anne's lap, wrapped her pink arms about her. 'Daddy, Aunty Anne is come in the night!'

Anne hugged her. 'My Fay! My Fay!'

'Who is this, Daddy?'

That little girl turned to me with her father's eyes, brown as a ship under a blazing sun.

'Her name is Eveline, my little one.' He drained his cup. 'But who she is, I do not know.'

More footsteps, heavier upon the stair. A woman followed, fair like Fay, handsome and pale. She held tight to a babe, wide-eyed with smiles to see us.

'Jessica...'

Anne moved towards the woman, but she looked only to me. For she had been listening, I knew, to our tale.

'Wine has dulled your true senses, husband. I know who she is.' The woman moved to the table, and Peter put a hand to her. 'She's a witch.' She looked me straight. 'Aren't you?'

All looked to me in that room of candles and wood.

And it was as if Mother looked to me too. When I shouted at her that I hated her, that I did not want her way. When I left her. These people looked to me for an answer. I would not have her a monster upon a parchment. They would know what a true witch was. I owed her that.

'Yes,' I said. 'I am.'

And Fay jumped to her father and tugged her mother.

'There's a witch in our house!' She pointed to me.

She laughed as I looked at them all, this family who saw me for what I was.

A witch in their gentle home.

22

'May I take Henry?'

Anne reached for the babe in Jessica's arms, his fat fingers clutching for her.

Peter poured for his wife, as she stood looking to me.

'Are you a witch too now, Aunty?'

Anne laughed. 'How you have grown, and just look at your strong brother!' I watched as she breathed his smell of milk and sleep. 'Here, sit with me, so I might whisper you secrets.' What a good witch she was.

I looked to Peter's hand in Jessica's. They were close, strong, these two. Good people. A good family. And now a witch was among them. But this family had a witching way, I had seen it. For that there was more to say, so I would say it.

'What do you know to be a witch?' My voice stirred them from their watching.

'I know! I know!' Fay rocked upon Anne's lap. 'A witch knows magick and healing spells and speaks to animals!'

'That is well, little one. And who told you these things?'

'Mummy did. Didn't you, Mummy?'

Jessica sat to the table, her husband's hand still in hers. Did they hold each other for fear of me?

'When Henry was born, I fell very ill, into fever and there was none that could help. Our priest—'

'Do not talk of that man!' Peter growled. 'Bumbling Catholic fool. Salvation for your soul indeed. I could have boxed his ears!' He swigged fiercely, muttering a curse.

'But then, husband,' her voice soothed him, 'a woman came to our door. She had heard our trouble.' Jessica looked me straight. 'She was not much older than you. She worked to heal me. I could not tell you what I drank, what poultices she made day and night. But my fever passed. She healed me.'

Peter kissed her hand. 'She did, and it is not God we thank.' He raised his cup. 'It is your kind, Eveline.'

Shame crossed my cheeks. I could not do what that young witch had done.

'I am not like that,' I said firm. 'I only seek balance. To right the wrong upon my family. That is all.'

Peter leaned forward. 'But these men you seek are dangerous. Armed. The trial will be thick with crowds…' The wine made his words tumble together. 'Will they not be looking for you? How will you reach them, fight them?'

'I will find a way!' My anger blew the candle flames. 'As I swore it on Mother's life as they took it! So I swear it now!' And I reached to my bag, pulled the stone free, and brought it down hard upon the table.

Peter watched the stone roll to rest at the bowl of apples. 'What is that now?'

'That, Peter Merchantman, is my mother's scrying stone…'

'Oh, it's so pretty!' Fay reached for it.

'No, Fay!' Jessica swept the bowl from the table, dashed apples about the room.

'Don't worry! I will get those naughty apples!' And the little girl ran to the shadows.

The stone sat upon the golden wood and the flames caught its grains of sparkling light. Jessica had moved so swift, without thought, a mother protecting her young.

'Think you my mother's stone is dark magick, Jessica Merchantman?'

'No… No, I'm sorry. I see that you are Anne's friend. But Fay is my child.'

She stroked that child's head, as Fay on tiptoe pushed the bowl upon the table. Then dropped two apples that rolled round its wide rimmed mouth.

'One, two apples...'

'Anne, your mother,' Peter started. 'I remember as a boy, she had a stone like this...'

Anne nodded and smiled as Henry bit her hair.

'And how you played with it, Peter. Telling the future. All our futures.'

He nodded, a sailor adrift on his memories.

'Three apples, four apples, five...'

Fay's hands felt for the bowl and sent those apples falling back and, *thank you, oh, thank you*, went the bowl to be so filled.

'These witches at trial,' I said. 'Are they gone bad, like an apple rotted,' I stirred the bowl, 'that turns another, till all are bruised and bitter?'

Peter swigged. 'There are stories, but...'

'Tell me.'

'That there are three girls among the accused. They were taught some magick, that they used to bewitch a man... they stole a newborn... were seen dancing by a fire, but...'

'Who taught them?'

Peter frowned. 'An older witch, people say, but...'

'Six apples, seven apples...'

Fay's hands moved quick. The apples spun about the bowl.

How like Dill she was, lost in play as she sang beneath her breath.

'And what do you think, Peter Merchantman? Of what people say?'

'One for Daddy, one for Mummy...'

Good apple, bad apple. Good witch, bad witch.

'These are stories to keep us locked up at night. This war with the king has brought suspicion at every door. That my wife, like many others should be saved by a witch, but then sudden they are hunted. Why is this?'

'One for Aunty Anne.'

She smiled, but I knew she was sad to see Fay's father so.

'This militia, this Jacobs is full of bloodlust. The will of God, ha! While we watch, guilty and toothless...' He looked to his blade and gun. 'Mark me, there is a bad apple in this town, and it will rot us all!'

Peter tipped the flagon, and found it wanting. He stood to seek another.

'Husband...' But Peter only stroked Jessica's arm as he swayed.

'And this last one for Aunty's friend, Eveline the witch!'

Anne caught Fay for a kiss. 'What a helpful daughter you are!'

Again I saw Dill in the little girl, her silly games, her gifts of roots and berries and leaves with stories aplenty on them. And I was so gruff with her, while she danced on.

Fay pointed to the stone again, looking to her mother.

'See it is not bad, Mummy. I will be careful.'

'It is Eveline's, Fay.' Jessica looked to me. 'You must ask her.'

'Eveline, please may I hold your sky stone?'

I laughed and brought the stone before her. 'Scrying stone. And, yes, you may, little apple. Perhaps it will tell you a story.'

Fay held the stone, so large in her little hands, and she closed her eyes.

'I see something…'

Peter filled the cups again, sleepy now with drink that slopped and spilled.

'Your father? Rich as a king?' he slurred.

'No, Daddy, I see a girl… she is thin and has long dark hair. She is older than me… Oh, she is… she is so sad. She is crying and—'

I snatched the stone from Fay. My hand shook.

'Evey, what's the matter?' Anne was near.

'It is nothing. I am minded of my own sister. It is nothing.'

Jessica drew Fay to her lap, brushed her curls. 'Where is she now, your sister?'

Sweat was upon my lip. 'I... I took Dill to my own aunt. Mother told me to take her.'

What a liar I was. Mother wanted us both there.

Jessica stopped her brushing. The candlelight still in her eyes.

'Your sister's name is Dill?'

And her face grew bloodless.

'How old is she?'

'Some nine years and more. Why, Jessica Merchantman?'

'I think... I think that I saw her today.'

It was as if I had dropped to an ice-cold river, the water stopping my heart.

'What?' Making me gasp for air. 'Where... was this?'

'It was outside the jail,' Jessica spoke in a rush. 'A cart bringing more of the witches. I saw a girl, thick black hair, skin and bone. She was pushed over by a guardsman.'

Her shaking voice filled the room, and she was all I could see.

'She fell in the mud and a strange boy came to help her. He kept crying her name. "Dill! Dill! I will help you, Dill!" He kept on. The boy was troubled, in his mind...'

I held, watching Jessica's face, her lips moving, she spoke within my head, whispering above the beat of my blood.

'The soldiers, they hauled them up and brought them inside the jail, and the boy kept shouting, "Don't hurt Dill! Leave Dill alone!" And I thought how strange affected he was, and how different this girl's name, that he kept shouting over.'

I felt faint. Sick.

'Were there others with them? A woman with long grey hair? Did you hear any other names? Mabel? Tally?'

'None.' Jessica shook her head, as she rocked the sleeping Fay. 'I am sorry, Eveline.'

Anne was by my side, the babe upon her shoulder. Peter's eyes were sober.

The coven must have been hunted and found.

'Where is this jail?' I whispered.

'You cannot go there, child!' started Peter.

'Tell me now!'

Peter shook his head. 'It is too dangerous.'

'South Street. Four streets west of here. Beyond the square.' Jessica looked to her husband. 'For the children, Peter. For those children.' And he knew he could not stop me, for would he not do the same?

My hand shook as I picked up the stone. Bile rose to my throat. I must get to air. Dill was here. Dill was here.

I stepped to the door in the far wall, the high musket and blade pointing the way.

'Evey, wait.' Anne laid the babe in Peter's arms.

'No, Anne – not this time.'

'Evey, I can help.'

'No. This is my doing. I must go alone.'

Her eyes shone, she shook her head. My dear friend.

'I swear to you, Greeneye, I will return, I promise—'

I stopped. I had said that word to a sister who had trusted me. And to Mother. Both I had promised. Both I had lied to.

So I said no more, feeling the cold of the latch as I lifted it. I looked one last to their faces. Then I turned, and I went into the night.

Dill. I am coming.

23

The night air was chill upon my cheeks, as I stood, listening.

No crowds teemed. No children ran shrieking. No horses clip-clopped. Nothing stirred, but what echoed in my mind. Dill sobbing to me, not to leave her, please. Please.

I gritted my teeth to it, and moved from doorway to doorway, the wall at my back. Laughter bellowed within. A tavern, its drunks all at sea, sailing the long night. I moved on. Shuttered lights from slumbering houses lit my path. But I could see no square.

I remembered my first hunt with Mother. I had fretted so to catch the prey, to not shame her. And she had put her head close to mine.

Evey... Breathe slow...

I did. Deep, and slow.

Feel the wind...

And like her breath upon my cheek, I felt the wind pluck straw pieces from the ground, dancing them along as little old men, tumbling under her fingers.

So I followed those swirling straw men down the street, to where it curved, and grew wider still, showing shop fronts. The wind dropped, the straw men stopped. The square was silent. Waiting.

'Thank you, Mother.' I crept on.

The market was bartered to bed. Stalls and boxes lay like boats upon an empty shore. But as I moved, I spied the flicker of a lantern.

I crouched to a stall, listening, feeling the wood rough beneath my fingers. No sound.

I passed a water trough, breathed its smell of cow and dung. Something moved in the light. I reached a stack of boxes, and around one edge I peered. My breath held.

Beside a glowing lantern stood a great frame, nailed tall and strong, a long bench beneath. There, one aside the other, swayed seven ropes. And at their ends, like seven mouths, hungry for the day, hung seven nooses.

My fingers dug to the box, splinters biting.

The gallows.

Under my shaking grip, the box tottered. I watched it slide, too angry to care.

It fell with a crash.

'W… wuuh! Who…?'

From beneath the gallows stage rolled a pile of rags.

A beggar turned and saw me.

'Lady?'

'The jail,' I hissed. 'Which way? Tell me!'

With a trembling finger, he pointed across the gallows to a narrow alley in the darkness.

'There,' he whispered, unblinking. 'Follow there.'

Nearer I stepped. 'How will I know it?'

'Beacons…' He grasped for words. 'About the door!'

Then he fled, rolling, scampering, skidding through the stalls, and was gone.

I had not meant to scare him, but I could not help it. It was the sight of the gallows under lantern light, left for all to see and be afraid.

The wind came whipping down the alley. I lifted my nose, like Mother taught me.

Can you catch her scent, Evey?

I breathed in. Dust. Straw. Muck from the market. And there, I smelled smoke.

I ran. The clouds drew back from a slender moon, curled upon her bed of stars, and beneath her naked light, I reached a crossroads. Which way?

Whichwoo!

An owl, a beautiful white queen, perched high on

the houses. Her eyes glinted, as she steeled to hunt. Her beak nipped the air.

'Would you lead me, your majesty?' I whispered to her across that silent street.

This way, this way!

She rose, the feathers of her wings brushing the moon.

'For I am lost!' I cared not who heard me. 'I seek my sister!'

Follow, then! Follow, follow!

As her grateful subject, I flew in her wake, and together we crossed streets, and turned corners, till finally we landed with a flutter. She hooted soft, talons tapping stone, and I turned to follow her bold gaze. Yellow light was beyond the closest corner.

Slow I edged round, and I felt the heat before I saw them. Four beacons blazed upon a corner house, with bars across its shutters. The jail.

I looked back to cry the owl thanks. But she flapped and took flight.

Danger! Danger!

And then I heard what startled her. Marching boots, coming closer. I drew into a doorway.

'Hold up now! Hold up!'

The patrol was back, dogs padding for home.

'At ease, all of you.'

A door clattered open. I held so still.

'Up to quarters now. Till my order at four bells.'

I flattened my back, my heart knocked to the wall.

Men muttered, shoved and shuffled.

'Not you, lad, you're on watch.'

A deep growl of a voice.

Boots on stairs, yawns and coughs.

'I've been on my feet all night, Captain!'

'Stow that bellyache, Caldwell. Rest when you're dead, boy!'

My fingers scratched the wall. Caldwell. His musket had smashed her skull. The jail door slammed. Their voices murmured. A laugh on the stairs. I closed my eyes to think of Mother tumbling over and over.

And I fought not to shout for her, as all grew quiet.

The jail was closed, its flickering beacons hissing guards of flame.

Caldwell was within. His captain, that rumble of a voice. Meakin. I was sure of it.

They were here. And Dill was here.

Know your mark, Evey.

Mother and I had watched the deer drinking, breathed their musk across the water.

Choose one, then wait.

I came for my sister. Yet I swore revenge for Mother.

Choose one.

Was Tall One there too? His sleeping throat pulsing with life?

I could only crouch in the darkness. And wait.

'Three bells,' cried the town clock. *'Three bells, and all is well.'*

We shall see, old clock, we shall see.

The wind tugged at my cloak, as I stole across the street. Mother's stone weighed in my pocket. It was no blade, but it was something.

The flames from the beacons blazed fierce, as I stood before the door. My hand trembled as I knocked, the wood was hard upon my knuckles.

I heard a chair pushing back.

A hatch opened and Caldwell looked out, a frown upon his boyish face. 'Who goes there?'

'I do.' I coughed and brought Lady Jane's voice to be. 'I am Lady Jane.'

'What do you want?' Caldwell chewed on a tear of bread.

I stepped to the hatch. 'I want to see the prisoners.'

'You want what?' Gobbets fell from his mouth.

'To see the prisoners.' I leaned in, and Jane whispered those sacred words. 'The witches, sir.'

'Are you drunk, my lady?'

'No, no, sir.' Jane put my hand to her soft laugh. 'My father promised I might see these monsters for myself.'

His eyes searched about me as he chewed. Jane held my tremble still.

'Who is this father who promises such things?'

With a sigh, Jane raised my head. Would Caldwell see Evey watching him?

'Why, Lord Whitaker, sir.' I moved closer. 'The presiding judge at the trial.'

Caldwell's hand faltered upon the open hatch.

'Lord Whitaker?' He peered out. 'Do I know you? You look familiar...'

Evey shrank back. Jane had to hurry. About his thumb a ring of dried blood.

One of those little devils bit me! I will see her hang for it.

Dill's bite.

Turning Evey's scratched palm from sight, Jane reached and brushed her fingers to his, ever so slight.

'Are you one of the brave men who captured these wicked creatures?'

The boy watched Jane's finger circle his sore wound.

'Aye, that I am, my lady.' He licked crumbs from his lips.

'And,' Jane's sweet purr played him like the cat that pawed the mouse, 'are you to attend on the day, to protect us all?'

'Aye.' Bread caught and made him squeak. 'I'll be there, my lady.'

'Oh, good,' she breathed and made his colour rise. 'Then, if you let me see the prisoners undisturbed, perhaps we might meet after the trial?' And we both watched Jane press to his shaking hand.

Gulping his bread, Caldwell closed the hatch, and quiet he drew the bolt. He was smaller, standing alone before me. A candle dripped in his hand. The mouse blinked to the cat.

'Hurry, my lady, the captain will skin me alive if he hears.'

So Jane entered his nest, brushing Caldwell close, so that he caught the scent of her, quivered with wanton fear of her.

And I quivered too as the door closed. For I wanted him, his neck between my jaws.

The room was small and full of gloom, above a single lantern cast weak shadows. Two doors I saw. One ahead, one barred with a long stave.

Dill was in there. She must be. I must draw this mouse further.

'This way,' he whispered.

And Jane followed and watched him raise the heavy stave with a grunt.

'We must be quiet, my lady.' Caldwell put a finger to his lips and winked.

I swallowed.

'Where is your captain? The other guards?' Jane whispered, as she moved behind him, and watched him place the stave near the door.

He motioned above. 'Asleep, the lucky dogs...'

I trembled. Yes. Dogs, they were.

I watched Caldwell open the cell door and raise his candle to the dark within.

'These witches don't half stink, mind.' He held his thin nose as he stepped through.

'Then we must be all the quicker, dear heart.' And I stood on the threshold, as I felt Jane's hand reach for the stave.

Caldwell winked again, the candle above his head, gasping in that foul air.

'Where are they?' Jane placed her hand upon his narrow back. 'I cannot see them...'

And with her other, she lifted that heavy stave quiet behind me.

'In the far corner, I'll be bound.' He turned about in the blackness.

'Show me.' Jane raised the stave high. 'I must see them.'

As he turned away, showing her the back of his head. 'You're a strange one.'

Jane swung that stave so swift that it hummed before me, and it struck Caldwell such a blow that he dropped like he had fallen fast asleep.

His candle rolled into the dark cell.

'I am, brave boy.' Jane pursed her lips. 'Stranger than you know.'

And then with all our strength, we hefted again to stove Caldwell for good, cleave his skull, like he did Mother's. To kill—

'Evey, stop!'

My swing stayed.

The candle rose into the air, and beneath it came a grubby hand, then a pale face in the tallow light.

Dill.

24

'**D**ill!'

My whisper fought to shout, straw slipping beneath my feet as I ran to her. Dill stood in the candlelight, her dress muddied, her legs scratched and bruised.

'How did you... Are you hurt?'

I drew her close, breathed her smell of meadow grass after rain.

'No, Evey.' The flame moved in her still eyes. 'I am not hurt.'

I smoothed her hair. 'That is g...' My words caught, so happy, so guilty. 'That is good.' I smiled. She did not.

'Dill, listen—'

'Pass the candle there, Dilly.'

A hand reached from the gloom.

'Here's the wick, Alice.'

The candle was held to another, and as its flame passed, the room grew brighter. And I watched as, some standing alone, some huddling, those shapes became women. Two were old, gathered to that guttering flame. Three near my age. And holding to one of those three, a young lad who rolled his eyes and hummed. The women looked to me and to Caldwell upon the straw. Then their voices came all at once, like the dead whispering to life.

'He'll wake soon enough.'

'We must go.'

'I can't run.'

'What of the guards?'

'They'll come.'

I felt for Dill's hand.

'We must hurry, Dill.'

'Whuu…'

'He is rousing,' said a girl, a cut upon her brow. 'Bob, come with Beth now.'

She pulled the boy as he hummed.

'Dilly come? Dilly come…?'

'Well, I can't run nowhere.' The one called Alice sat heavy to the wall.

'Nor I, Jessy.' The other joined her, like two gnarled roots against the stone.

Dill shook off my hand.

'I will stay with you, gentle mothers.'

'No, you won't,' coughed Old Alice. 'Get you gone, young 'un.'

My heart pulled as Dill shunned me. But she must come.

'Dill, I'm sorry, but we—'

'Sorry?' She rounded to me. 'They killed Spring for your sorry! They threw her to a flames!'

The candle shook.

'After you left me.'

Her voice was harsh. Something turned in my mind. A dream of flying and flames.

Caldwell groaned. Tighter I gripped the stave.

'Lizzie, Mary, come!' said the girl Beth. The others tarried, scared to run, scared to stay.

'Dilly. Those men.' My voice cracked to whisper. 'They shall pay, I do promise.'

'You do promise!' Dill stepped to my face, her breath hot. 'What good are your promises, Evey?'

'You don't understand, Dill.'

'You lied to me! Tricked me!'

Anger rushed through me. Was I not there to get her? She was not listening to me.

'I had to, because you're a silly mite always tarrying and dancing…'

'Better than you, who don't understand the stone what you took.'

I bit my lip. The stone was sudden heavy in my pocket.

'Dill, we don't have time—'

'Better than you…' she sneered. 'Who don't know no magick! Who— Ow!'

The women gasped. I hadn't meant to slap her. It just happened.

'Dill, I'm sorry.' But she struck me away.

'Those men didn't kill Spring,' she coughed through tears. 'She did it. She gave me to the witch hunters.'

'Who is she?'

'Who do you think? The one you were so thick with. Our aunt.'

My bones turned to ice.

'Grey?'

I felt the cell turn under my feet.

'They have a pact.' Dill held to her cheek. 'And Grey's waiting…'

She looked so angry and so sad. I was too stunned, too guilty to touch her.

'For you, Evey. She said she's waiting for you.'

I felt my legs sway. A pact with Tall One.

My head spun in that dank room. The world was upside down, tipping too fast. Caldwell shook his sore head through the straw.

'He wakes and he will bring the others!' Beth stepped quick. 'Come now who can!'

She pulled Bob around Caldwell's waking body.

The two girls followed. The open door beckoned, and I took Dill's arm, cold to my touch.

'Hurry, Dill. Don't let us—'

'I will go with them. With Bob.' She pushed my hand away. 'Not you.'

The candle burned in her black eyes. Mother's eyes, furious to me.

'Please, all of you!' Beth hissed from the open door.

'Dilly come! Dilly come!'

Bob sought Dill among the cobwebs, and he smiled as she found him. I do not know whether it was envy for that, or anger at Grey, or the hurry that made me do it, but I grabbed to Bob's other hand in a rage.

'Fine, Dill! If you will not come with me, then let us go with your new friends!'

And I pulled that strange boy so savage towards the cell door that his body jerked.

'Evey!' Dill stumbled after.

'Funny, Dill!' Bob laughed as I pushed him through the doorway, as Beth too pushed Mary and Lizzie into the room beyond.

'Stop!'

Caldwell stumbled to his feet. As he lunged, Beth tried to swing the door, but he caught to it, flung it wide with a crash.

'Captain! They escape!'

Shouts thundered down the stairs. And the girls screamed, as tight I held to Bob, as he clutched to Dill, as we all rushed across the room.

'Bring the light down!'

Beth pointed, holding to the laughing boy. The guard door opened. Meakin's face, full of fury. High I swung the stave.

'Stop there!'

And struck out the lantern, pitched that room into blackness.

The girls' hands were upon me, pushing, pushing, desperate to flee.

'Out of the way!'

Soldiers crashed into the room.

'Get them!'

'Stow your sword, fool!'

'I have one, Captain! I have one!' Caldwell cried so brave.

And sudden Bob's hand was torn from mine.

'Dilly! Dilly!'

'Get off him!'

Blind I flung about and found Dill's thin frame, grasping her good.

'Give me that musket!'

'Let go!'

'Dill, it's me!'

Bodies tussled and fell through the screams and shouts. Then a sharp pain, teeth sinking into my hand. White light in the dark.

'Ah, Dill!' I let go. 'No!'

She had bitten me. She had bitten me.

'Come on!' Beth pulled me through the jail door.

'They're escaping, Captain!'

'Caldwell, out of the way!'

'Dill!' I reached back in the dark but my stinging fingers found nothing.

'No! He's my friend! Leave me alone!'

'Go!'

'No…! DILL!'

But Caldwell staggered into the beacon light, the boy Bob smiling under his arm.

He grabbed me and he laughed like he laughed when he killed Mother.

'Evey! He's going to fire!'

I swung the stave wild.

Fire spat from the dark. Heat blasted. Blew Caldwell out.

'I have the musket! Run!' Dill cried out.

'Get this devil off me!'

And Caldwell, brave Caldwell, lay bloody, laughing no more.

'Run, Evey! Run!'

'Dill!'

I struggled, but fear of death made those girls too strong, as Beth kicked the door shut. And then we were outside the jail. The rain was falling hard. And the girls were pushing me forward, pushing for freedom.

We ran for our lives.

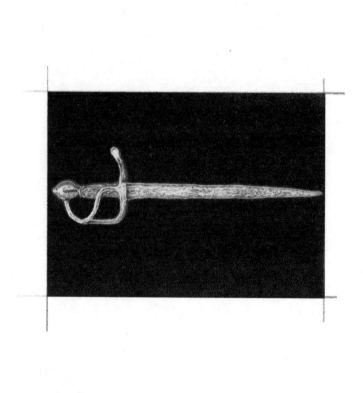

25

'Come on, Bobby! Faster!'

Beth pulled her brother along, as she pulled us all, her hand tight to mine.

'Moon!'

Bob cried to the sky, as our feet slapped to the cobbles, our hearts beat, our breath gasped, but none was louder than Dill to me.

You lied to me! Tricked me!

On I ran with those girls I did not know, through a town I was lost in, from men who had taken my family, and now betrayed by our own blood.

Grey's waiting for you, Evey.

Mother's sister. Why had she done this? Why?

'After them!' I heard Meakin's shout. 'Or you will hang in their place!'

But no answer came on those echoing streets. We could only run.

'Rain!'

Bob cupped his hands to the silver drops and faster we sped, past houses blind and dumb. We were witches in the night, and witches were not welcome. Help a witch, hang with a witch.

Ahead the roads crossed, each way to emptiness.

'Mary, Lizzie.' Beth shoved to the girls. 'Go different ways…'

Fast behind us they came, shouting.

'Go now!'

They bolted like rabbits, Mary to one silent street, Lizzie to another. Beth pulled me on. My chest ached, a taste of iron on my tongue, as the rain soaked us.

'They split! You, and you! Go around, hurry!'

And Meakin's men answered with a holler, the streets filling with their cry.

'Give that here!'

Through the rain, I heard it. Metal clicking, locking.

'Beth, get—'

A shot rang out. Rushed through us. Beth tumbled to the wet stones.

'Ah! My leg!'

A slash of red burned her thigh. I kneeled to it, but she cried out.

'Go on with my brother…' Bob hugged his sister. 'Please.' And she tried to push him, but he only held her tighter. She looked to me over his shoulder, blinking tears and rain.

'Dill loves you very much, Evey. She ever spoke of you.'

My chest clutched as those shouts pounded closer. I had tricked her, hurt her.

'They are coming now! Go! Go! Make it right with Dill.'

I turned and ran as Beth held on to her waving brother, and I sobbed mouthfuls of rain as I slipped and pushed for all I could.

I made the corner, when a cry came hale and hearty.

'Take them!' Meakin's voice barked, and Beth wailed.

'Evey, run!'

'Pick her up, I'll take the mooncalf.'

'Let him alone!'

'Get them back to the jail! Leave this last one to me...'

Then I heard the steady step of one pair of boots. One who hunted me.

'I won't lose you a second time!'

My fine captain and I were alone at last. My fingers itched for a weapon. I wiped the tears away. Must think.

Those streets all looked the same. I needed cover, quickly.

'It's you, isn't it? The one from the gate?' His burly shadow swaggered and swayed. 'Your kind call you a warrior. Well...' And I heard the sigh of his sword drawing. 'So am I.'

I darted to an alley, where barrels clustered to the walls, and I ran its length. It was blind. Rain jumped from the rooftops. The wall was to my back.

Slow those footsteps came on, and I watched Meakin's shadow stop. I crouched low to a barrel and held my breath.

'I know why you are here, girl. But it won't do no good.'

He brushed the water from his bristled head.

'They should never have trusted your kind. His bloody plan, not mine.'

His sword sang in the moonlight, rain testing its edge. His plan. He talked of Tall One. Anger made me rise, and I hurled my words at him.

'My family never aided your war! My mother was a healer. And you killed her!'

There was no more hiding. For where could I go? I was an unarmed girl, and he was a big strong soldier. Yet he could not see me. Not yet.

Meakin sighed as he stepped closer. 'Mark me, I was for taking her to trial... But bad things happen in wartime, child.' And he raised his hungry sword to sniff the shadows. 'That Grey witch of yours, she knows best of all.'

'She is not mine, curse her wicked ways!'

My heart beat with the rain that drummed those barrels. Meakin took a step forward, when I heard a whisper amid that wet darkness and the stench of stale beer.

Do not be afraid, Evey.

And Meakin's shape became like the stag, coughing in the damp air.

Slow your heart.

'Fret not, little one, since it's just us, and you're going nowhere... It's true, the witches helped rout the king who hides from their damn magick...'

Breathe with him.

Quickly I tore shreds from my skirt, knotted them fast to my fists. 'But when this Grey has helped us find you all, she will die too. Master Jacobs will see to it.'

He knocked a barrel.

'I will see to it.'

Feel your blade.

I had none. But I had the stone. My fingers found it, waiting in my cloak. I gripped it, my palm ached.

'All witches must die. There can be no trace of their foul work in God's new kingdom. Now...'

His sword scraped the wall, coming closer. Closer.

'Do not be frightened.'

Harder I gripped. Mother's stone. Mother's stone. Mother's stone.

'I will make it quick!' His laugh shook the shadows. 'My little warrior.'

Enough. He did not hunt me.

Now, Evey.

I leaped from my lair, over the barrel like I jumped through the woods, and I hurtled towards him, like I ran for the stag.

'Ah, there you are…'

Meakin raised his blade.

Keep a light tread, on your toes.

The cobbles under my feet, cold as river stones, towards that drinking deer.

Meakin swung up.

Your prey will leap, and you must follow beneath.

'Come to me.'

I drove low.

The blade hummed above my head.

I reached and found a finger all alone. I snapped it like a dry stick.

'AH!' Meakin howled like the hound he was. 'You bloody animal!'

Feel their fear.

He swung wild, a rage of dark upon dark.

I rolled, as his sword bit the wall, spat sparks of white and blue.

'Blast you!'

Taste their scent.

I jumped up, the stone in my grasp, and I threw my fist, hard and fast.

The stone smashed his jaw. Teeth flew.

How my fine captain screamed in pain and fury.

How he sought my skull.

I dived to the ground, feeling the metal skin my back, and kicked up, drove him heavy to the wall, punched the breath from him.

My hand throbbed as I stood, as Meakin stumbled for breath.

Time your move, dance with your prey.

'I w-will,' he hawked blood, 'kill you, witch!'

I had to get above him. I raised the stone, made to leap for the wall, when sudden the clouds drew back, and the moon threw her light upon the rain, upon us.

'I see you, my pretty! There!'

Meakin lunged. I twisted. Too late.

Ice. Hot. The blade sliced my side.

Meakin grinned his bloody grin and hefted high.

Fire through my side, I drove my fist up.

'There!'

Metal struck the stone against my palm.

His eyes bulged, sweat beaded his hair.

I grasped the blade in my knotted hands, held it fast as it writhed.

'Clever girl.'

He grunted. I fought to turn that trembling blade.

'But you,' as it shook between us, 'will... not...!'

As he bore down upon me.

And I screamed through the pain, through the rain and the light.

For Dill who I had wronged. For Mother who I had failed.

I screamed and screamed and drove to this grinning sweating shouting man.

'GIRL, YOU...'

As I pushed up. Up. UP.

'WILL... NO—'

Meakin stopped his shout.

I knew why. His blade was buried deep in his mouth.

He slid away with a last sigh, eyes wide.

'I will, Captain.' Pain seared my side. 'And I did...'

Make your prey good, feel its death, Evey.

I felt to his neck. I closed his staring eyes. I smelled his scent of sweat and blood. And I thought of the stag that lay at our feet by the running river.

'He is dead.'

I could not stop shaking. My side was on fire.

The rain was cool on my face. I leaned to the wall. So tired.

Squeaking below me. Two rats watched me back.

'Don't... be... afeared. He was a... dog, see... who... killed...'

They scurried away.

'Mother.'

I gasped in the blackness.

The alley had grown longer. Its walls rolled beneath my palms. I was sick, bile bitter across my tongue.

I wanted to cry, but my side hurt so.

I had to get to Dill.

Dill loves you very much, Evey.

I fell. Barrels rolled.

Dilly loves you!

The ground was cold, but it did not move.

I could rest a moment. Only a moment. Then I would be

right

Dilli'msorry

D

I dreamed of her.

How we hunted.

I dreamed of the doe that leaped through the mist.

How we crept closer.

I dreamed of the great stag that roared from the white.

How it charged towards her.

I dreamed of her swinging.

How it struck.

I dreamed of running, leaping.

How my blade flew.

I dreamed of the stag's eyes burning.

How it screamed and fell.

I dreamed of finding them, fallen beneath the trees.

How he lay twisted, how her leg was torn.

I dreamed of smelling her sweat.

How she gripped my hands, grinning with pain.

I dreamed of her wiping my blade, wet to my cheeks.

How she whispered in the still. 'Now, my daughter, you are a hunter.'

I dreamed of her shaking, as she kissed me.

How alive we were.

I dreamed of Mother.

26

Sunlight's fingers prised my eyes, heavy with sleep.

I saw beams above, white walls all around. Blankets lay upon me. I moved, and pain pulsed. I felt to my side. It was bound tight and scratched and itched. And as I drew breath, so I heard another breathing. I turned and there was Anne, sleeping close from a chair. Her hair smelled of rainwater. And I remembered.

I will kill you, witch!

Moonlight on the rain. Rats.

Blue sparks in the blackness, as steel struck to—

Quick I turned, gasping at the pain, as I looked about.

The stone sat upon a little table, light sifting its silver grains. Then I remembered more. How I had fought with Dill.

How I had struck her. And how I had lost her.

Scuffling at my feet. A giggle.

Up jumped a doll, all raggy and woven. Her hair was red threads, buttons for eyes that looked about a land of blankets and sun.

Up jumped another. A wily crow, with feathers stuck, and a beak of painted black.

Two little hands held them, this Raggy Lady, this winged beast. They looked to me, then bowed to each other.

Quickly the crow flew forward, but Raggy Lady leaped away, and a voice said, 'Why do you chase me, sweet crow?'

She jumped as the crow snapped,

'Because I am Death, and I am hungry for you!'

Yet Raggy Lady shunned his embrace.

'I am not your worm to peck.' And she feinted as he flapped.

'You will be mine, I say!' that crow croaked and spread his wings wide.

'For I am Death! I am your Dea—'

He held, caught in time. He coughed, he choked, he clawed his feathered throat.

Raggy pointed straight, for her spell was cast.

'Fie! You curse me!' he mewled, waving weak. 'But I love you so!'

Then he fell to twitch and turn, then twitch no more.

The lady bent and gently, gently she kissed Death's

beak then she danced into the sun and with a laugh she was gone.

'The End!'

Up Fay leaped, a giant above her stage, her curls bouncing bright.

'Did you like my play, Evey?'

'I did, very much. But tell me, what is the name of this fine Raggy Lady?'

I stretched, pain coiled tighter.

'Eveline!' Fay's eyes shone. 'Though she likes me to call her Evey.'

'Oh, like my name, you mean?'

'She is you!' The little girl laughed. 'Silly Evey!' And plucking up Raggy and Crow, she skipped them from my bed to the window bright with morning.

'Yes. She is you,' said a voice. 'Silly Evey.'

Anne's eyes met mine, and my heart leaped like a raggy doll in the sun.

'Fay woke when Peter and I brought you in,' said my friend, as we watched her humming niece. 'The child knows a fight when she sees it. She played the nurse, helped me clean and stitch your wound.'

I winced to sit, my teeth grinding.

'How did you find me?'

'The owl, Aunty! The owl!' cried Fay, flapping her fingers. 'Oh, it was beautiful, Evey! It woke me up!

Toowittoowhoo! Toowittoowhooo!' She hooted and laughed.

'I have never followed an owl before,' said Anne, 'but Peter and I found you. And you have fevered through a day and a night, Evey.'

I looked to her. 'What? Then I must go! The tri—'

'The trial is a few hours yet. Save your strength.' Her fingers were cold as snow's first touch.

'What of Meakin? Did you see him?'

From the window seat, Fay showed Raggy and Crow the great world beyond.

Anne nodded. 'We saw... his body.'

'He was one of the four, Anne. Of Tall One's pack.'

She stroked my bloody hand with its cuts aplenty, its mark of Dill's bite.

'Did you find your sister?'

I thought on how Dill held her cheek where I struck her.

'She would not come with me. I got angry and...'

And I thought on her glaring to me. How she shouted as I pulled her.

'Surely she wanted to escape, Evey?'

Fay whirled Raggy and Crow. Like Dill playing by the hearth of home.

'She does not trust me no more. I left her see, with Grey, our aunt. And...' I fought the anger and shame welling in me. 'Grey betrayed us – they parleyed Dill to Tall One.'

'The Witchfinder?' Anne started. 'But… why?'

'To save themselves. Meakin said that witches helped to battle the king.'

Anne watched me, her gaze as sure as that day I met her.

'And now Grey helps them hunt those witches.'

'This damn war,' whispered Anne.

'Dill said Grey is waiting for me, but all I have to fight is this, Greeneye!' I snatched up the stone and laughed, made the pain writhe in me. 'Mother's stone which I took from Dill. Because I knew it would hurt her!'

'Evey, calm yourself.'

'She made me so cross! Always talking of it. And Mother. I was so angry with her going on. But I didn't mean it. I just wanted to get away! I didn't know they were going to come! I didn't know!'

I buried my face in my torn hands, as Anne stroked my sorry head.

'Evey, your mother loved you.'

'I have to get Dill back, Anne. I have to make things right!'

'And you will.' She gripped my hands. I felt Meakin's sword, turning in my fists.

'We will find a way, Evey. We will.'

I looked to Anne, her fingers pressing mine.

And to Fay, little feet drumming the floor.

To Jane's dragon dress waiting upon a hook.

And I thought of that painting in Anne's home, her mother's hand upon a scrying stone like the one I grasped in mine. What Mother had said about the women in her family.

They have a witching way.

'Why do you join me, Anne Greeneye?'

She smiled sad, waving to Fay and Raggy.

'For my sister's sake, Evey. I join you for my sister.'

I opened her palm and I placed the stone there. 'What was Jane like?'

Anne watched as I turned it.

'She was like you, Evey. Fierce and soft as one. A wild thing, but gentle with me. And she was gifted, knew healing, knew the trees, the land, like my mother. I loved her. And I was jealous of her.'

That word, *gifted*. How we envied our little sisters.

'Because she knew magick?' I spun the stone on Anne's white hand.

'No,' she laughed. 'I envied her taking a lover, for I never had, and she was the younger... And my jealousy scorned her, told her Sir Robert was not to be trusted.'

'Sir Robert?' I held the stone still.

Anne's smile trembled, as she nodded. 'He was with her that day.'

Fay started at the window, leaning closer.

'He discovered Jane's witching way. Told her to stop as I listened, a jealous sister at her door.'

I drew my finger across stone.

'But she only laughed at him. Told him that no man would rule her. That their play was ended. Then she took her horse and rode to the woods.'

Fay pointed, all curls and cheeks.

'Aunty Anne! Evey!'

But Anne was lost to the story of that day.

'And Sir Robert rode after her in a rage. To any who saw, wild Lady Jane was riding too fast again, followed by a fretful lord. But I knew better.'

She steeled, as her memory ran to catch those horses.

'I was scared, jealous no more. I followed them and I heard Jane laugh at him, and then...' Anne shuddered.

'I heard her scream and I stopped running. And...'

'Oh, please, come and see! Please!' Fay cried.

'He came from the woods, holding Jane in his arms, shouting for help. And I knew from her head hung loose that she was dead.'

'Oh, Greeneye.' I reached to her.

'I knew, Evey,' she whispered. 'I knew he had done it. He told all she fell and broke her neck. But I knew better. I knew the awful truth he buried in those woods.'

A single tear from Anne's cheek dropped to wet the stone.

'Father would not listen to me. He said my mind was full of childish stories. And I lived on in that house with that man a friend to my father, too blind to see the women he loved.'

Fay jigged Raggy and Crow in delight.

'Greeneye, I am sorry for it.'

'No, Evey,' she said sharp. 'Too long these men have made me doubt, made me weep, made me feel sorry for my mother, my sister, for myself. But I will not have us sorry any more. Swear, we will fight against those who try to trap us, to hurt us, to kill us!'

Her green eyes blazed with the fire of her being.

'I do swear it.' I kissed Anne's fingers curled about the stone, and I thought of our mothers, watching us, willing us.

'They're coming! Oh, they're coming!' Fay came running, her face flushed. 'There's a bear, tumblers, there's people, so many. Come and see!'

She drew away my bedclothes and I rose for her pleas, holding steady to Anne's arm. Smiling her little smile, Fay offered the window, like another play for us to see, and music came to the air.

'The bear is so funny!'

I knew what this was, what came rolling so merry into town.

A lute. A fiddle. Laughter.

People were everywhere. Some watched a tumbling man, drawing cries as he fell. Others a great brown bear in a cage, muzzled and moaning. Children sniffed the smoke that rose from grouse on spits, or ran among the stalls, through colours of red and blue, green and gold. All around crowds chattered and laughed and hollered as one.

Fay pressed Raggy to her face.

'Look, look!'

She pulled me so gentle, for she knew I was pained about.

'Players, Evey!'

Holding to Anne's arm, I leaned forward, Fay's curls brushing my chin.

Upon a stage was an ugly crone cloaked in black, with a mask of nose and hair and teeth. The crowd booed. They loved to fear the witch, and quailed at her talons, her billowing cloak, her teeth that would tear their skin. Then another player, a soldier, strutted to that stage. Long was his hat, bright was his sword. He stroked his yellow beard and weighed his keen blade. I knew this brave form, like it was that first day I saw him.

With a smile, that player looked around and spied us at the window. He lifted his hat and blew a kiss.

'He sees us!' Fay squealed then. 'Who does he play, Evey?'

'Why, my little apple. He plays Tall One. The hero of the day.'

And I his Raggy Lady, ready to take the stage.

'You're not too tired to go, are you, Evey?'

I laid my bloody hand upon Fay's hair and I looked to Anne, her fist closed tight like mine around the stone, around our mothers' hearts.

'Oh, no.' I smiled aside my pain. 'Not never.'

For there were such sights to see this day.

This fine day of the Trial of Those Foul Witches.

27

Sweat came to my brow as Anne helped me down
the stairs. Jessica and Peter Merchantman stopped
their talk as one step, two steps, we made our way.

'Mummy, Daddy! Have you seen all the people and
the bear, and the spinning men?'

Fay ran to her father's lap.

'A bear, you say?'

'Grrrr!' She curled her hands to claws.

And, 'Grrr!' Her father bared his fierce jaws.

'Don't eat me, Daddy!'

'But you are so sweet! Grrr!'

Anne eased a chair to me. My fingers felt the smooth
wood, but I did not sit.

'Thank you, Peter Merchantman. For what you
did. I do not remember…'

Rain and darkness drenched my memory.

'We were glad to.' He looked to Jessica. 'Now, there
is time yet to eat…'

From a bubbling pot, Anne brought broth steaming quick and good.

They watched me. Ready to catch me. Even Fay stopped her humming as I stood and supped my soup. Rosemary, garlic and there, arrowroot to draw my pain. Anne had healing skills, like her mother. I drank down the dregs, as from the street, came the roar of the bear. It was like my summons.

Holding my side, I moved to the door where Jane's cloak hung next to her sister's. Lady Jane had shrouded me well, tricked that boy Caldwell, laughing with the dead. But they would be watching for that scarlet lady now. I needed something more.

'I want to go with Evey!'

'Fay, be good.' Behind me Peter's voice shook. 'And I will take you later.'

Like I shook.

'But, Daddy, I want to go with Evey.'

'I said no, Fay.'

A sigh, then a rush past me and Fay was reaching for her father's hat. She placed it solemn upon her bright head, her smile was as broad as its brim.

'If I cannot come with you, will you dress up with me, Evey, before you go? Please?'

She ran her fingers along the big hat that smelled of her father. I thought of when Dill and I played ogres, rubbing bark upon our monster cheeks, red much about our glowing eyes.

'Quickly, little one.' I stroked her cheek. I was her Raggy Lady and this day was my crow.

Fay clapped, then went spinning about the room. She brought her father's great coat, more hats, a rope belt, a shawl and my bag, till the table was piled.

'Will you dress up too, Aunty?'

'Why, surely,' laughed Anne.

'Mummy, may we use your paints? Please?' Fay tugged Jessica who frowned.

'My paints for your games?' She wagged her finger.

'Please.' Fay looked from her mother to me. 'I want to be the witch. Like the play.'

Then Jessica laughed. 'And you will have them, Fay, for they are all our things.' And made quickly up the stairs.

Fay bade me sit at the table. And slowly I did, for my want to please her was greater than my pain.

'You will be the old witch,' she said. 'And I will be the young one.'

Fay brought her mother's shawl, and as she did, a thought came whispering.

'In my bag there, you will find another. May I wear that one?'

She pulled Mother's wool shawl from the bag, beads tinkling to be free.

'It is so lovely, Evey.' She drew it across my shoulders, and Mother was fast about me. Only one witch would I be in this dread play.

'You will be Evey's sister, come to visit,' said Fay to Anne, bringing the other shawl to her aunt. 'And now,' she sang out as Jessica set a box grandly before her, 'I will make your faces!'

She threw it open to the treasure inside, circles of white paste, red, gold and blue.

And there, among those colours like flowers to the fresh sun, a plan unfurled. I saw it grow true. How we might venture to the trial.

We would go as what they feared.

We would go as what they would never forget.

We would go as those foulest, wickedest witches.

'I will make you the good witch, for you heal and help.' Fay daubed Anne about her cheeks with white and gold paste.

And as I watched, something more came to mind. What Dill said at Croake Farm.

Ash is for binding, Evey.

I moved to the hearth, feeling the baked heat. As Fay painted Anne's cheeks, so I reached to the embers, and felt the ash through my fingers.

Ash is the binding, Evey, between life and death.

Mother's song of making and mending.

From ash we rise, to ash we fall.

'Yes, Mother,' I whispered as Fay drew rings of red about Anne's eyes, as the good witch came to be.

From ash we rise. I brought my fists to my face, grey ash coating my skin.

To ash we fall. And thick I covered my brow, my neck, my mouth.

To ash we all will go.

'Look!' Fay pointed to me. Like a spirit waiting to be seen.

Jessica gasped, as look they did.

'Evey is the bad witch!' Fay came laughing to my arms. 'For she is as wily as a crow, as hungry as a hunter!'

I brought that little girl to my embrace, and I wanted her to be Dill, and to think I had not tricked and lost her. But I had done those things. So I could only force the fierce shame from my chest, and bow low to that kind family with all my wicked, jealous heart.

'And my trial awaits,' I hissed, smelling the fire upon my lips.

'Oh, you are perfect, Evey! And so are you, Aunty Anne.' Fay clapped over to see us. We were her witches, for she had made us so.

The sound of lute and pipe came from the street. Death waited beyond that door, croaking in that music. It was time.

'Greeneye. Are you sure?'

'As sure as anything I know,' Anne moved to me, 'Eveline of the Birds.'

She reached for my hand. Hers so smooth. Mine so gnarled and cut.

'My good witch,' I said. 'My dear Anne.'

I lifted the latch.

'No, Evey, not yet!' Fay stayed my arm. 'Not yet! Please! I want to play more!'

Peter Merchantman rose, and swept Fay into his arms. Louder she cried against her father, and stretched for me, pleading, kicking. And Jessica watched them, hands to her mouth. She cried. Like her daughter cried. And my throat burned to cry too, for their kindness to me, a stranger in the long night. Peter had braved patrols, given me shelter. Jessica had fed me, made me warm. And Fay. How she had charmed me, the wisest witch of all. But they were not my family, who once I fought to be free from. These people had shown me how lost I was without my own.

I brought her fingers to my lips.

'Fay, listen. I must find my little sister.' I held her gaze so blue, like a jay's feather. Like a clear winter sky. 'You were right, when you saw her with the stone. And now Dill needs my help.'

'I like her name,' Fay sniffed, tears forgotten.

'That is good. I gave it her when she was a babe.'

How scared I'd been then. That Mother would love me no more.

'Will I see you again, Evey?'

I put my fingers to her chest, felt her heart dancing.

'You will, little apple. Here you will keep me, always.'

'You have magick, Evey!' Fay looked to me full of wonder. 'You can see my heart!'

I kissed her fingers one last. And as I did, I felt a song rise in me, that Mother would sing, rocking Dill to sleep.

'Close your eyes and find me,
run to the wood, and hunt with me,
follow the birds and fly with me,
dive deep and swim with me,
close your eyes now and find me.'

Fay's eyelids drooped.

'Goodbye,' I stroked her sleeping cheek, 'my little witch.'

Peter reached behind the door, a wooden cane in his hand.

'To keep you steady,' he whispered through his daughter's curls. 'Two blades lie slumbering. Turn forward to wake the mother, who is strong and steely.'

He touched its rounded handle. 'Turn back to loose the daughter, who is swift and deadly.'

A weapon. To keep me steady.

'Thank you, Peter Merchantman, you are a good man. I have not met many.'

He laughed softly, winking his farewell.

Jessica pressed something to me. 'May God be with you, Eveline.'

A cross on a small chain of black beads. Upon the cross a naked man pinned in pain.

'I do not—'

'My god, Evey. Not theirs.' She folded my fingers around the beads. 'My magick. To help you.'

I turned my back to Peter Merchantman, to Jessica, to Fay, feeling their sadness like burrs caught upon my cloak. Then I opened the door and drew back the curtain on the day.

28

The crowd, that many-headed creature, reared before us, belching smoke and shouts.

I tasted bitter ash.

'Evey.'

People lurched against me, and I winced.

'I will fetch the horses.'

'Nay, Anne.' Her painted face watched me. 'Horses will not bring us close. We must stay on foot and act our part.'

I swallowed the pain, as I swayed before that river of people. But my good witch pushed against the throng.

'Make way there!' She raised her long arms. 'Lest the Devil take your souls!'

Two men turned and laughed to see us so.

'Ho ho, make way for the witches!' cried one, bleary with beer.

'Your trial awaits!' The other bowed low.

'It's working.' Anne bent close. 'They think us part of the revelry.'

So we hissed and we glared, and the crowd laughed and swept us up and along, into its sights and sounds. Rabbit on spits, turning my stomach. Tumblers flashing red and gold. Children pointing, laughing. Women selling witch dolls, with little nooses.

Then beneath it all, those clamouring mouths, those gasps and shouts, I heard something that made my skin prickle.

Caw! Caw! Caw!

Hawkers bellowed and beckoned, yet I saw not them.

Only wings, feathering the light.

'Goodly players there, will you champion this fierce beauty against these hounds?'

A bear caged and chained. Two dogs barked beside her. Their master's smile yellow as their fangs. The crowd drew in, yet I followed that falling shape to the shadow.

A crow lit down, looking for me.

And Dill's words came flying from that night at Croake Farm.

It is not a gift, Evey. I only like animals. And they like me.

'Come, my pretty witch!' cried the master. 'Come cast your spell upon a wager!'

'Why, sir!' Anne opened her claws. 'We witches do not gamble on lives.'

Birds do, if you let them.

That black bird blinked.

But I think you do not try to, sister.

I felt to his nape, smoothed his jet throat.

'Why would we wager, sir?' Anne's mask creased to a smile.

And I smiled too, to remember a ridge, a soaring lord of the air, and my sister and me.

You know the birds, Evey...

'And I know you,' I crooned to him. 'Like you know me.'

The good witch threw her arms aloft and cried.

'When we witches can take all that we desire!'

The crow stirred. Circling on high. His kin crying.

Dill was right. If I tried, I could do anything.

The crow opened its beak, as I opened Peter's blade and pressed to my wounded palm. Pain woke, as he eyed me, as they cawed and cawed.

Try, sister! Try! Try!

So I did. I felt for the stone, and I clasped it.

The good witch grinned. The crowd jeered. And I reached.

To his black beak, his black tongue, his black heart. Feeding on mine.

And I wanted to weep for it all.

If Mother could see me now, casting a spell. For I had found my witching way at last, in the flight of a crow.

Hungry like me.

The master banged the bear's cage. The crow rose into the air.

'Come, then, another! Who will wager before the trial?'

Angry like me.

Anne's arm hooked mine, and she pointed ahead, as the bird flung to the sky.

Magick like me.

'Evey, the square!'

The crowd swelled as we passed along a narrow street, with buildings dark as wet sand, and windows watching. Those buildings seemed to part ways, like arms spread to show the walls set about tall curved doors. A cheer rent the air. The crowd stopped its murmuring and stretched its many heads. There it was, that thing of death, that only men make. Seven mouths hung open, with two lower, for little necks.

The gallows waited.

'Evey, the crowd is so thick. We must look for another way out of the square.'

We could go no further. And we could not go back.

But there. Beyond the gallows, I spied an archway.

When the time came, there was a way out from this foul place.

My heart beat in my mouth. My tongue was so dry. My wound ached.

And like she sensed it, Anne's fingers crept to mine.

'Evey, do you know what you will do?'

Try, sister! Try!

'I can help… If you tell me.'

I looked up. A cloud was gathering.

'You will help, Anne Greeneye.'

I sounded so sure. Yet my stomach churned. I had never done this before. And there was something else. A fluttering in me, like feathers. I was excited, for what I had done, for what was coming.

'We will know the moment, I promise you.'

A cheer burst around us, and we turned to see guardsmen shove and shout, as they drove a path from the gallows, through that eager crowd, towards the great doors.

A bolt shot.

Those doors swung open.

And the trial began.

29

The doors swung open, knocked dust from stone. The crowd surged, pushing Anne aside, washing me with pain.

'Evey!'

'I'm all right!' I gritted my teeth. 'Do you... see Dill?'

'Somebody is coming.' She heaved against those bodies. 'I see—'

'I see him!' A shout behind us. 'I see the Witchfinder!'

And through the weaving heads, I saw what they saw.

A man stepped into the light and raised his arm to the cheer of the crowd, in command of his world. He moved with a smile through the shouts and calls, and how I ached for him, my Tall One.

In his wake scuttled a man of the church, black hat and black book, who looked not to the crowd, but set his gaze to the gallows for there were souls to save this day.

'My father is coming.'

I turned to see old Lord Whitaker, unsteady of gait and grey of hair, bound in a fur. At his side, frowning through beetled brow, strode his friend, his trusted liar, Sir Robert. My friend breathed fast. I knew she saw her sister dead in his arms and, like her, I heard his lies through the noise of the crowd.

Climbing the stage, Tall One passed so close to me. How comely he was, with eyes brown as a buck hare, long hair yellow as straw in the sun, and skin shorn and pale as morning mist.

People pushed to see, their jeering weight upon me. I cried out with it.

'Evey, we must turn back—'

'No! I am lost.' I reached to her through the swarming madness. 'I broke my promise to Mother! Because of me, Dill is here! I must put it right, don't you see?'

Worry etched her painted face, but Anne saw it good. My sweet sprite of the wood, who had envied a younger sister. Who saw Jane's fate too late. Those sad green eyes saw it good, and ever would.

In fury, she looked to Tall One upon his stage. 'Evey, you are never lost! I am with you!'

As this hero pulled to each the nooses, and with each pull, the crowd cheered.

'No,' I whispered. 'This will not be. I will not let you, you hear me.'

But Tall One did not hear me, as he bowed to Lord Whitaker, his skin all sallow and bloodless. Winter would take him, I smelled it.

He drew a roll of parchment and looked to the mob, and it calmed like a child hushed for a story.

The old lord coughed to clear his throat, and then he began.

'On this day of our Lord Almighty, as your appointed justice of the peace, I hereby decree that this trial will properly show...'

He swallowed and shook, his voice was weak as his body.

'Show the wicked abandon of the accused, and will show how these people became enchanted and so enchanted others in the pursuit of their own...'

He coughed, then coughed again and again, each echoing louder about that still square. Sir Robert came quickly.

The crowd murmured, as all watched Sir Robert bring him to his chair, watched as Tall One took the scroll and sent his words soaring above our heads.

'In the pursuit of their own pleasure, their own gain, their own nefarious desires.'

Then, as a thought came to him, he curled away that parchment. He knew his lines, like a liar knows his own heart.

'For we all know they are witches, good people! We know what they are about, do we not? They have bedeviled your lives. Cursed you, harmed you, made you suffer. And for that, they must pay for their wickedness, their treachery, their wilful crimes!'

Fingers pointed, eyes glared, mouths shouted in a chorus of hate. My fingers ached for my hidden blade. To scythe them, like wheat for the harvest. But not yet. Not yet.

'And this trial shall call witnesses, true to this fact.' Tall One raised a hand, as he played on. 'To bear statement against the accused, it will show their wicked vices...'

The crowd cheered.

'Their intent at destruction.'

The crowd cheered long.

'And their bedevilment of you!'

The crowd cheered over and over and over.

He played them all. This pale wolf. This smiling dog.

'And what, what, my good fellows, my brethren...'

His voice was so quiet, holding us all.

'My brothers, my sisters, my children – tell me, what do we do with witches?'

'Hang them!'

'Hang them!'

'Hang them!'

'Good people, your patience is rewarded!' Tall One cried. 'For the witches are coming!'

Slow they entered the square. Swaying and shifting, pushed and pulled along, a stumble of women. Some old, some young who aided the old. And herding them, guardsmen with muskets, like shepherds prodding their flock to market.

The crowd gasped and pointed.

Then I saw what I had been waiting for. And my breath stopped.

Two children walked along the path through that baying crowd. They were holding hands. One was a boy who nodded over, smiling and waving like this day was his. The other was a girl who looked ahead, spite the cries and the laughs and the cursing, as that happy boy swung her hand. She reached out gentle to an old woman, lost in the noise. She raised her eyes to the gallows, and stepped towards them, a boy in one hand, mad as a hare, an old maid in the other, blind as a worm. There she was, brought to this trial, this terrible day in this terrible town. Because of me.

My sister.

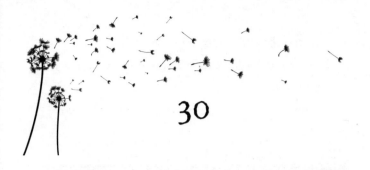

30

'Make way, make way there!'

Four soldiers held high their muskets like oars to cut those waves of cheer and jeer. While all shoved and shouted to catch a sight, we made the edge of the crowd, and saw them come, those so-called accused.

First stumbled the girl, Mary. Her hair was pulled, her clothes ripped and muddy, one eye folded to a bruise. Then Beth and Lizzie, both white as chalk. Old Alice, Old Jessy, bent to follow. I knew their names. Dill had made sure of that.

The boy, Bob, waved to the crowd, his tongue lolling like a pup's, his eyes roaming the sky. He smiled, for his good friend whispered to him, and she stroked his hand so he knew she was there. She looked steady climbing the stairs amid the screams, her eyes bright through that dark nest of hair.

'Dill!'

I shouted, but so did everyone.

'Don't they look hungry?' laughed a man. 'Here you go, witch!'

An apple smacked Mary's face, broke brown and slimy.

'Please!' she sobbed. 'We did nothing!'

But no one could hear or would listen, as more things flew and the women raised their arms against a rain of food and straw, mud and more.

Anne held me fast, but through my pain, beyond that swell of bodies, I saw something. The crowd had been so hot, pushing to the square, that a space had grown behind it. It was the way. I knew it, like it beckoned in the sunlight.

'Anne, I see it.' I laughed aloud and brought her head close. 'You must go, quickly!'

'What do you mean, Evey? Go where?'

I turned her painted face. 'Bring the horses. Bring Peter. All of town is here. But those streets are clearer. You can circle round, back to Merchantman.'

She looked where I pointed, towards the street that led to the jail. A few people ambled to watch, yet it was not choked heavy by that stinking, hollering, endless mob.

'Peter? But... will he come?'

I turned to the gallows where Tall One strode his stage, as he cried, 'Tie them!'

And I watched as those women, a shake of hair and bruises and tears, were turned to face the crowd. Watched as soldiers moved along their line, pulling hands, tying fast. And there, beside Old Jessy, was Dill holding to Bob's hand. He waved to the crowd, but a soldier came and pulled them rough. I watched Dill wince, felt those ties cut my own wrists.

'He will come.'

I watched Bob look to his bound wrists. No more could he wave at the people, nor swing high his friend's hand, and so his smile fell, and tears shone in his eyes.

'Peter is a good man.'

I watched the crowd heave hungry to the gallows.

'For there are none here, Anne Greeneye.'

I watched Tall One bow to Lord Whitaker. 'My lord, we wish to call the first witness!'

And I held Anne's face to mine. 'Come riding fast to the square. When I hear you coming, I will know to get Dill.'

'But... how, Evey? How will you get her?'

I stroked her cheek, feeling the paste that Fay had painted. How far we had sailed from her land of play and light.

'Dearest heart,' hissed the bad witch, 'I will give them sights such as they have never seen. Nor will again.'

I hugged my friend close.

'Now you must do the same, my good witch,' and I breathed her in. 'Bring them your sister, Jane. Bring them the magick that I see in you!'

Madness frothed around us, but we held together, an isle amid those crashing waves, as her eyes caught and flickered green flame, so Anne smiled.

'I will do it, Evey. I will do it for Jane.'

Her cold hands shook to mine.

'And for Dill. And for you.'

She kissed me, warm and quick, then she turned and pushed through the crowd, her shawl flying loose, as she spun between bodies, slipping out of sight.

'Come back to me a true witch, Anne Greeneye,' I whispered. 'For I know it is in you, as it was in your sister. As it is in mine.'

We were all sisters, our hands joined. I saw it clear, like the sun that burst upon that dark place, and Mother's words flew to me, like the talons of an owl stroking my head.

For my blood, your blood, your sister's blood.

On that day I had meant to leave my family, for I thought I was not like Mother and Dill. But that day lit the fire that burned so fierce within me. I had used ash for binding. I had made blood magick with a crow. I had found my witching way. And it felt so good. Now

I must finish my spell, and become a true witch, like my mother, like my sister.

With such joy, such knowing in my heart, I turned to see the doors open. And there among the witnesses, walking towards the stage, towards Dill, towards me, was an old woman, stooped and bent.

It was Grey.

31

Mother once told me you must be still when you see a snake.

So I did not move, as Grey hobbled, playing the crooked woman with the crooked back. I did not breathe, as she leaned to her cane and climbed the gallows steps. Only my gut curdled, as all around me cheered, and I watched Grey bow to the court.

She betrayed Mother, her own sister.

She gave Dill to Tall One.

She hunted her own kind.

She was guilty, and for that I would sentence her.

Yet like the worm in the apple, truth wriggled in me. I had been glad to be rid of Dill, to leave her with this woman. And my shame was bitter, like pips in the rotten core.

She had tricked me, cloaked in care, like her guise now. She had done it to spare her own skin. But something more gnawed on my thoughts. That night at the coven, why had she let me go? Why was only Dill given to Tall One, and not me?

'Look! It's our Tom!' Someone pointed.

A bearded man, heavy in paunch, stepped among the witnesses.

A chill ran through me. I knew him. I had seen him in a dream, when he stumbled drunk about the coven's fire. They were all there. Tall One, Grey, Mabel, Tally. But I had cast that vision aside, as my fevered guilt for leaving Dill. Yet there he was.

I gripped the man before me. 'Who is that there?'

'Why, are you thirsty, witch?' laughed his fellow.

'That's our own Tom Barrow,' he breathed beer. 'He owns the Red Lion.'

They turned back as two women climbed the stairs, and I felt the cold in my gut turn to ice.

The coven witches. Mabel with her pretty curls. Old Tally, her temple scarred where Dill had struck her with the stone. To think I had scolded her for that.

'Pray, quiet, good people!' Tall One brought his palms to the air. 'Let us hear the testimony of these summoned witnesses.'

Like a creature brought to heel, the crowd hushed.

'You!'

So swift did Tall One turn, his boot squealed and made poor Mabel start. The crowd chuckled to see it. How well she played the timid maid.

'Tell the court your name, girl.'

'I... I... am Mabel Harding, sir,' she stuttered to the watching court.

'And tell them, Mabel,' Tall One circled, 'what have you lost that was so precious?'

Mabel shuddered. Hidden was her quick way, her laughing eyes.

'My... my child, sirs. My newborn...'

The crowd muttered over. For shame to lose a newborn.

'But it was taken from you, was it not?'

'Y... yes, sir...'

The crowd moaned.

'And do you see here, among the accused, the one who took it from you?'

Mabel shook, curls covering her eyes.

'Yes, sir. Yes, I do!'

The crowd gasped.

'She did! She took my babe! She did it!'

And Mabel flung her lie across the gallows. To Dill. Who never hurt no one, who liked to run and play, and ride horses in the moonlight. Who sang to dogs she found, and made friends in the darkness of a jail cell. Who looked now to that crowd shouting to her, its cries sounding over and over, through my aching wound.

Tall One raised his hands. 'And do you see any here who helped this wicked child?'

Mabel nodded firm, those curls shaking loose.

'Them did. Them old bitches there!'

Her finger flew to Old Jessy and Alice, huddled as chickens feared of the fox.

'They said they were midwives, but they tricked me!' Her face aflame, so hot she stoked her tale. 'After the birthing, they stole my babe while I slept.'

'No!'

The crowd cried, shaking its fists in the air. And as they pressed, I felt the stone against my body as though it nudged me to be free.

'But this is not all, good people!'

Tall One turned to face Tom Barrow.

'Sir, declare yourself to the court!'

The man picked at his beard. 'My name is Tom Barrow, sir. And, your honour.' He bowed to Lord Whitaker who nodded so grave.

Tall One turned. 'And you are the landlord of the Red Lion tavern?'

'That's right, sir, on the road from town,' and the Witchfinder waved him on. 'Well, I was after putting the barrels out not a week ago, when I saw a light in the woods…'

'What kind of light?'

'A fire, sir, a big one! Such a heat from it!'

'And you heard singing, did you not?'

'I did, sir.' Tom Barrow flicked his eyes to the girls, Lizzie, Mary, and Beth. 'It was them girls there.'

'And did you see what they were doing, Tom Barrow?'

He looked to the girls again and they looked him back. 'They were after dancing, sir.' He picked slow those bristles. 'Around the fire.'

'Aaah!' Tall One lifted a finger to the air, tugging the tale to be. 'And tell us, was there something strange about this dancing?'

Tom Barrow coughed.

'What was that? Speak up, man!'

'They… they were naked, sir!'

The crowd hissed and Tall One grinned, teeth glinting.

'And what did you hear above the singing and the spit of that great fire?'

Tom Barrow turned to Mabel, who shook and shook. How good she was.

'I heard… I heard a baby crying, sir.'

And louder and louder voices shouted from the crowd.

'They took her child!'

'Those girls are witches!'

'Shame on you!'

I closed my eyes to my mewling side, to the clamour around me. Perhaps this was a dream only, and I would wake from it, and Dill would be free and Mother would not be dead.

'We are not witches!' A young voice came above those shouts.

I opened my eyes. No, this was a nightmare. And I must awake to stop it.

'He lies! That Tom Barrow is a liar!'

It was Lizzie, her cheeks streaked from tears.

'We were on the road home.' She trembled to point at that bearded man. 'And he came at us from the dark! He was drunk. He tried to... he dragged Beth to the woods! I hit him with a branch. We had to fight him off and run... He lies!'

'You bloody lying... pig!' Mary screamed and she ran head down for Barrow.

But a soldier was faster, and caught Mary, locking his arm to her neck. So easy it was to grab girls. Had Tom Barrow done the same with Beth that night?

But the crowd loved to see this soldier bring a wild witch to heel. He pulled her by the throat, and Mary wept with fear and rage, that the world mocked her, that she was a woman, that a woman was never stronger than those men who drag them to the dark woods.

Tall One stepped to Tally. Time for her part in this tallest of tales.

'Old woman, did you see Tom Barrow attack these girls?'

Tally shook her head and smiled her empty smile.

'No, I did not, sir. But I was in the tavern when Tom Barrow returned all a'frighted. Saying he saw them girls. Oh, he was a shocking sight, sir.' And she placed a bony hand upon him. 'As God is my witness, he does not lie!'

The crowd cheered for that. *He does not lie.* Yet he does, Tally. Like you. Like Mabel. Like Grey.

'Why would you believe him?' sobbed Lizzie. 'Because you drink his bloody beer?'

The soldier shoved and she fell crying to her knees.

Witches must be brought low and taught a lesson. The only lesson.

'We have a final witness.' Tall One pointed to Grey, who waited, as a spider in the shadows. 'First make fast these wild things! Raise them!'

'Raise them!'

The crowd echoed.

'Raise them! Raise them!'

With pushing and pulling and curses, two soldiers hauled those women to stand. A stool became a step, and one by one they were made to climb upon the bench, dragged by bound wrists along its creaking length. And how the crowd laughed to see those seven swaying, and there in the middle, smallest of all, my sister Dill.

She bent her head to Bob, her hair brushing his cheek. She whispered something only for him, while all below licked their lips, stomped their feet.

The pain at my side throbbed over.

Mother. I am frightened. I do not know if I can do this.

'Quiet, good people,' shouted Tall One. 'Our last witness is old and frail. We must give her space to speak!'

He offered his arm to usher Grey, what a dread pair they made.

'Old maid, what is your name?'

'My name is Mary Tell.'

The crowd became a hushed thing, straining to hear.

Mary Tell. Did Grey choose that name to taunt us?

And with a start, I knew it, as I watched her mocking tremble, her crooked way. She knew I would be here, watching. She was taunting me like a knife between my aching ribs. She had let me go that I would follow Dill, as her bait.

Grey is waiting for you, Evey.

'And what do you do, Mary Tell?'

'Why, the best thing there is, good sir. I bring children to this world.'

The crowd sighed and Tall One spread his arms wide, beaming with horrid glee.

'Then tell us, Mary, as your namesake befits. Tell us what you saw that wicked night.'

32

'I saw them all, Master Jacobs! These girls. This boy who is not a boy. These all, I saw, as I see you now.'

Tall One frowned.

'How so is this boy not a boy?'

All looked to Bob, who sang to the passing clouds.

'It is a horrible, wicked thing I saw, sir.'

'And God must see this wickedness. Tell us, Mary!'

'Tell us!' cried the crowd.

So Grey slid her serpent tail about us and drew us in.

'I was on the road to town, returned from a birthing. It was very dark, there were no stars, no moon to see by. Soon I smelled beech smoke upon the air, and then I heard a crackle of flame from the woods. I crept towards that sound, and among the trees I saw a fire burning. It flickered and moved so strange...'

Her fingers reached, became those moving flames.

'On I crept through those trees. And when I felt

the heat upon me, I kneeled to watch, and there, Lord above, what a sight I beheld.'

Not a sound came, only Grey's voice curling above us, like smoke from that fire.

'I saw these women here. They were circled around it, dancing before the light. They were laughing. And, I feel shamed to remember it, for... they were naked all. Naked as the babes I birthed that day.'

The bench creaked.

Dill had turned and she looked to Grey.

Tall One stopped. 'But, Mary, this is not the end of the tale, is it?'

'No, Master Jacobs, it is not.' She pointed to Dill. 'For I saw this little girl...'

Her words dripped their poison to the crowd, who did not breathe, did not blink.

'I saw her. As clear as she is here. I saw her change this boy...'

Her crooked finger marked Bob. He smiled and nodded.

'And what, pray, did she change this fool boy to? A bat? A goat?'

'No, no, Master Jacobs. He was not...'

How she tussled with this story, so heavy upon her hag heart.

'He... He was not a boy when first I saw him...'

A gasp from the crowd. How now?

'Then…' Tall One leaned closer, the wolf smiling to the snake. 'What was he?'

Grey looked up to Dill. And Dill looked down to Grey. The wind blew soft, then—

'He was a pup, my lord.' Grey shook her lying head. 'That boy was a dog.'

Mutters and murmurs ran all about.

Tall One raised a hand. 'A dog, you say?'

Grey nodded so sad. 'A pup. I heard the girl, she called it Spring.'

Dill flinched. Grey had cut her with that name, that joy she gave to her dog as it barked to a bright morning.

For she is life, Evey! She is life!

Grey will pay, Dill. I swear to you.

'But how, Mary? How did she change a dog into this boy?'

Grey gave a sob. My nails dug to my palms. She will weep, I promise you.

'Tell us!'

'How?'

Shouts from windows high, from watchers low, from all corners. Finish the story, Mary Tell. We would know how, we must know.

'You must tell the court what you saw!' Tall One prowled. 'No matter the pain!'

'Pain, sire?' Sudden she glared to him. 'I have more pain than you or any man will ever know! Enough pain to pay for a kingdom!'

'Enough, Mary Tell!'

Spittle flecked his lips, his neck strained, his eyes were mad. What a man was this, who had come from a woman. He had been a babe once, tottering for warmth and love.

'Tell us, so that the souls of these women might be saved!'

Grey threw her hands high, as she birthed her lie upon that gallows stage.

'She took something from the fireside. I could not see what it was, for all the dancing, the shrieking. They sang louder, as the girl moved to the fire, and she held it above her head, and they danced faster and faster...'

'What was it, Mary Tell? What did she hold?'

'A baby!' Grey cried. 'Her child – the woman there!' And she pointed to Mabel, who gaped and sobbed. How long had they weaved this story of woe?

'And what did she do?'

'That poor babe. Oh, sir, how it screamed and wriggled to be free... She... She...'

'Say it, Mary Tell!'

'She threw it! She hurled that little life down! Into the fire!'

Mabel shrieked to pierce our souls, as she fell to her knees.

The crowd reeled and bellowed. Women wailed and wept. Men snarled and spat. Children clung closer. How wicked a thing was this girl.

'Shame! Shame!'

'Evil witches!'

'Born of the Devil!'

I could not move, trapped in a tempest wrought by her, that darkest thing of all, Grey who buried her face to hide her smile.

How I would smash her.

'Pray, silence!' Tall One raised his arms. 'We ask now for Lord Whitaker's counsel!'

Like infants shaken from their nap, the sitting men were roused to stand. The puritan opened his black book, eyes darting to its pages. What prayer could cleanse this wickedness?

Those shouts fell to seething quiet, as Lord Whitaker spoke.

'This day is a dread one, indeed. And my duty, as your magistrate, is heavy to bear... But we have heard the good and clear testimony of these brave witnesses...'

He motioned to Grey, Mabel, Tally, Tom Barrow. Such pedlars of lies.

'And... for this court there cannot be any doubt to

the foul crimes committed. By the power vested in me, in the eyes of God...'

The churchman muttered his barren prayer.

'By the will of the people...'

The people cheered to be so called.

'The will of this town, I must pass the sentence of guilty.'

'Guilty!' echoed the crowd. That word so good to hear.

'Upon you all and hereby sentence the accused... to the punishment of hanging by the neck until dead.'

'Hang them! Hang them! Hang them!'

At Tall One's bark, his guards pulled down the nooses, and guided their open mouths over shaking heads, till they settled on soft necks, like snakes slid to their nest.

Those poor women. Some looked down. Some cried to the sky. Some closed their eyes to it all. For surely soon, this madness would end, and merciful death would free them.

And Dill. She looked only to Bob and soothed him with whispers against the lust of the crowd, the heavy rope that scratched his cheeks.

It was nearly time.

With the one hand, I felt to my wound, and I lifted the binding.

I pressed. Hard. White light in my sight. My wound sang with pain.

The guards made sure of ties to hands. The bench swayed, keen to be kicked.

It was as if it happened in silence, though all about me cheered and cried.

Lord Whitaker lifted his shaking hand.

'It is with regret that I have passed this sentence. But it is the law of the land, and you have been found guilty of witchcraft.'

Silence then, only the lost moans of Old Jessy and Old Alice.

It was nearly time.

I felt for what waited.

'But before your punishment is enacted,' the old lord's voice scratched the walls of that silent square, 'it is the just will of this court that you may beg forgiveness for your sins and pray for salvation. Do any of you wish to—'

'I would speak now.'

All eyes turned to a white-faced girl with a black nest

for hair. She looked out to us from that groaning bench of the guilty, a noose so thick about her thin neck.

And as my fingers closed upon the stone, Dill began to speak.

33

'I am Dill.'

Her face was pale above that noose waiting to bite.

'These are my friends.'

Her voice clear, like a bell that chimed to call us in.

Tall One lunged.

'No, Jacobs!' Lord Whitaker cried and Sir Robert stayed him. 'It is her right. And my ruling. You wish to save souls, do you not?'

Tall One glared but stayed he did.

'Go on, young...' But the old lord could find no words for the girl who watched him. 'You may speak.'

It was time to finish what I had started.

'Thank you, sir.'

Dill smiled slight to him, and in that silent, falling light, she turned.

'This is Lizzie, there is Beth, that is Mary.'

Their tears shone as they looked to her.

'That is Old Jessy, there is Old Alice. This is my friend, Bob. He is not a dog.'

'But I do love dogs, Dilly!' The boy's laugh echoed about.

'Yes, you do.' Dill looked to Grey. 'And I love them too.'

Harder I pressed, deeper I breathed, wringing my pain.

And as I gripped the stone, I thought of eyes, so many eyes, blinking black.

I thought of feathers unfolding, rustling to rise.

Dill looked to the crowd.

'These things that were said. All that you heard today. Do not fret or be afeared…'

I thought of talons tearing air, beaks opening, cawing for me.

'They are only stories. Told to frighten you.'

She looked beautiful. Like Mother.

'Do not be frightened.'

Then up, up beyond the walls, to the sky I reached. And called them to me.

'My mother and my sister, and me, we ever looked to help people. Many people.'

Dill smiled, and it was like fish darting silver in the river. Like snowdrops pushing the dark earth. She smiled and I wanted to cry out to her, for she was my sister, and I would never leave her again. Not never.

'We helped some of you here, most likes.'

Some heads dropped or looked away. Wretched, wretched town.

Tall One moved, but Grey was quicker, like the snake she was, to stand before Dill, swaying above her crooked head.

'Little Dill,' she said, turning her knife upon that hated name. 'I knew your mother, little Dill.'

Dill looked to her aunt, so wily, so wicked.

'You told that man Jacobs, that Mother hurt people...'

'Why, yes, child, I did—'

'You told him we were dark witches...'

Grey nodded.

All was still.

And they were legion, gorging the light.

'You led him to our home that day. With his men.'
'Yes, child. I did. It is the law.'

A pall of blackness, a wave of wings.

'And you watched. You watched Mother die.'
Grey smiled her crooked smile.

So I lifted my palms, and marked my cheeks with
blood, the blood I gave to a crow.

'Yes, little Dill. I did.'

His brothers smelled me, sought me.

'But now my question, little Dill. Is it true? Tell
us… are you? Are you a witch?'
All watched. All waited.

And such joy filled us.
For the birds and I were one.

My sister looked out to that great sea of faces.
'I am. I am a true witch. Like my sister. Like my
mother, who you killed.'
The crowd gasped, reeled back, fear stuck in its throat.

Then a scream sliced the air.
Heads turned at the clatter of hooves on stone.

And, my, we were hungry, so very hungry.

I saw them. Fast down that path from the jail. Two horses charged into the square.

There rode Anne upon Coal, Jane's scarlet cloak like the wings of a dragon. High she held a sword, its blade a smile in the light, her face daubed fresh. My Greeneye. And upon Shadow another galloped, whirling a fiery beacon. It was the Red Goat, and he glared through that billowing smoke, through the screams of people who fell and fled.

'Stop, whoever you are!' Tall One shouted. 'Stop, I say! Men!'

But the good witch did not stop. She split that crowd asunder.

The Red Goat grinned and swung his flame above his red head.

'DILL!'

I loosed my hidden blade, felt it sing with glee, as people jumped away.

Grey looked to me. Tall One pointed to me. Blood dripped to my smile.

'I am a true witch! Like my sister. Like my mother. And I am come!'

I turned my blade to mark them both.

'For you.'

Then I laughed for what I felt fast in me, for what I had done, for what was coming, as around me whirled and swooped and screamed, with all their black hearts, a great and beautiful murder of crows.

34

'The birds! God save us, the birds!'

They were upon them.

Men swung by their feet.

Soldiers firing blind.

Women hung by their hair.

Children swept up, swallowed.

The air was choked with wings. Beaks pecked. Claws ripped. Blood ran.

Caw! Caw! Caw!

Everywhere people fled. All senses plucked.

Caw! Caw! Caw!

How the crows laughed, and how the crowd wailed, as a creature cornered. But not that way, where a good witch reared, and a Red Goat breathed flame. And never that way, where a bad witch cried,

'Is this not a great show?'

They wept. I screamed at them.

'Is this not a wondrous sight?'

They turned their bleeding faces from mine, hid their sorry heads.

But for one, who stood upon the gallows stage, with a look of longing for me. The girl he had missed that day, come to claim him at last.

'Kill her!' He swiped at that shrieking cloud. 'Kill that… thing!'

Soldiers dived into the sea of screams. One drowned, and his musket sank fast from sight. Another saw me, till his eyes were snatched. A third rushed the swarm of birds and raised his ready gun.

'Evey!'

Coal's hoof struck his jaw, his musket vomiting.

'Come on!' Anne cried, as the crows spun and swooped.

Through that chaos I ran. And I felt so alive, my wound beating, stone and blade in my fists. I grinned for the pain, and for the joy, as the crowd fell away, as they all howled for me. The stage was mine at last.

And there upon that bench. Dill. Her mouth shaped to shout. *Evey.*

I jumped the gallows steps where people wriggled like worms beneath a rain of beaks. They crashed against the stage as Anne leaped from her steed.

Tom Barrow said his prayers, but the puritan

man forgot his, and vaulted into the crowd, his book flapping with the crows.

'The witches are here, sweet players!' I cried. 'Your final act is begun!'

'STOP!'

Lord Whitaker cried shrill and stared to the good witch before him.

'Anne?' He stumbled upon the shuddering stage. 'Anne, it is you, isn't it?'

She looked to her trembling father.

'No, Father. I am Jane Greeneye.'

She strode forward, so tall and powerful.

'I am a true witch. Like my friend. Like my sister.'

Her blade turned to Sir Robert who sneered as the Red Goat whirled.

'Killed by him.'

'Killed?' he whispered, then he saw the murder in Sir Robert's eyes, that terrible truth.

'My Jane?' He looked for her amid the smoke, the wheeling birds. But his daughters were gone long ago.

Sir Robert leaped for Anne. But I grabbed him good, reeled him away.

'Evey!'

I turned to see Tall One lay his blade to Dill's neck. 'Take your hands from—'

'Good Eveline!' Grey sprang, a knife in her claw. 'I told you the stone would make you strong!'

I looked to it, her words cried by those crows.

A powerful weapon, Evey.

Was that a lie too?

'There is so much anger in you, Evey!'

So be it. I ran at her. She danced away, her knife stroked my arm, carving red pain.

'And look at your birds!' she cried to the clamour above. 'What a witch you are!'

Anne smashed the knife from her grip. Grey howled.

Mabel and Tally flew, talons out.

'Hold!' swung the Red Goat.

Heat hummed, his beacon burst fire about those wicked witches. Tally shrieked, shrouded in flames. Mabel, poor Mabel, her curls caught, she rolled away, a wail of smoke. Pretty no more.

'Witch! Watch your sisters hang!'

I spun to see Tall One kick the bench.

And the crows were more and more. Screeching, seething, tumbling.

And the crowd thronged, and the stage shook, started to split.

Again Tall One kicked. Again the bench shifted.

'Stop him!' cried Beth.

'Got you!'

Sir Robert grabbed Jane's cloak.

'Evey!'

Quick I balled my shawl, smeared it across my bloody face, hearing their cries above.

'Did you pull same at Lady Jane that day she died?'

He smiled at that. 'She was a lying wench! Like her witch mother!'

Anne twisted to be free.

And I hurled the shawl, Mother's shawl, upon this man, this liar who brought woe to women, who must pay for his crimes. This was my court, my sentence. I gripped the stone.

Sir Robert ripped the shawl away, and my blood wafted to the air.

And I reached for them, my feathered army.

'You fight like the girl you are!'

He pulled but stopped when he saw what came for him.

A great shape unfurling, diving, twisting. A crow made of crows.

They struck him. Over and over.

In his last, he saw Jane, who pulled her scarlet cloak from his grasp.

Before they took his throat. His scream.

I tasted his blood on my black tongue, such sweet revenge.

Their shape grew, bigger, blacker. Scrabbling for more.

Bird upon bird upon bird struck the groaning gallows.

'Stop!' I shouted, but they would not stop.

The world broke beneath my feet.

And in that terrible splitting I heard Mother.

Run, Evey. Now!

I started towards Tall One, the bench that he kicked and kicked.

'Dill!'

The broken stage lifted.

'Evey!'

My heart leaped as I leaped up that rising gallows.

Tall One tumbled.

And the crows were a teeming fury.

'Evey!' Dill cried out, her eyes huge with fright.

As the crows burst the guts of those gallows.

'No!'

Splinters flew, Tall One fell between the shattered wood.

Lord Whitaker tumbled, an old stick tossed to a stream.

'Hurry!' Beth screamed.

'The bench!' Mary cried. 'It's falling!'

'Dill! I'm coming!'

'EVEY!'

'Ev—'

They all stopped as one.

Legs kicked, hands wriggled, mouths gaped to breathe.

The nooses had them.

Now, Evey.

I ran.

And I jumped, high, high through the trees with Mother.

Bent through the falling air, pushing, willing my body to soar.

Stretched my fingers...

35

I seized rope.

It was Bob's noose, his face close, struggling to smile.

Dill swung beside him. Crows wheeled and spun and cried.

'Dill! I can…!'

I hacked my blade, such burning as I clung.

'Evey!' Her wrists wriggled free. She raised her arms, pulling from the noose. And smiled down to me, bright with life.

An arm curled about my waist, and my toes found the solid back of a horse.

'Evey, I've got you!'

'Anne!' I gasped. 'Dill, to me!'

She dropped from the rope and I clasped her body. She shook in my arms. I had her. But I could not stop.

'Anne, the others!'

Together we rose, the bad witch and the good, and together we cut those women free, Lizzie, Beth, Mary, Old Alice, Old Jessy, dropped them to gasp upon the splintered ground. Bob rolled to the earth.

'Dilly come?' he called above the din.

But his friend shook her head and smiled. He waved, as his sister pulled them into the fleeing crowd.

'Evey. I… I am sorry. I was so angry…'

'No, Dill, no, don't be sorry.'

And I began to laugh and sob so happy to hold her. I never held her like that, never felt like that, and it was good.

'Quickly! We must fly!'

Through a mist of tears, I saw the Red Goat point across the square, where people bent and bawled beneath that plague of crows who tore and bit and wrenched.

Caw! Caw! Caw!

Full of frenzy. Glutted with glee. Because of me.

'Ha, Coal!'

Anne clutched me close, and I to Dill, and her steed jumped through birds and the broken body of the gallows.

All that was done passed beneath us.

Lord Whitaker, a crow upon his still head.

Tom Barrow, his paunch split, life lifted.

Sir Robert, eyeless to the sky, his throat picked clean.

Tally lay in ash, Mabel in soot. But Grey, I could not see.

'Out of the way! Begone!' The goat flung his beacon at birds and bodies.

We charged across that shocked square, set fast for the far street.

'Greeneye! There!'

'I see it, Evey!'

CRACK!

A stall shattered to smoke. I turned back. Tall One reared upon a horse, threw his musket down.

'Another!' And snatched a gun from fumbling hands. 'Give me sight!'

'Quick!'

'Witch!' Across that carrion cloud he aimed. 'I see you!'

'Evey! Get down!'

I threw myself hard to Dill.

CRACK!

Death whistled above us. Dust and daub burst from a wall.

'Dill!'

I smelled smoke in her hair, as I felt her all about.

'I am all right, Evey.' I thought that musket had found her. 'I'm all right.'

'We're nearly there!' Anne cried. 'Out of the way!'

I looked to him, swearing to me. I have her now, Tall One. But mark me, I will have you before this day is done.

And I as thought on him, I breathed deep and turned the stone under my fingers.

'Hurry, fools!' He grabbed another gun.

Reaching for them, my bloody brood.

As he placed me in his sights.

Caw! Caw! Caw!

'Damn birds! Get away! Get away!'

He swung with his musket. But they swarmed and wrenched it to the air.

'They're getting away!' he shouted to no one, for his men were covered in crows.

'Through here!' The Red Goat cried.

We drove on, thundering by buildings and stalls and people.

At last we left that square, that terrible place.

The walls loomed as we rode. The Red Goat turned Shadow this way and that.

'How will we pass the gates, cousin?' Anne wiped paint from her face.

The goat ripped away his red head.

'Peter Merchantman!' I cried to see that gentle face, those clever eyes. 'I said you were a good man! And now a finer goat I have never seen!'

Peter smiled to me, then to Anne. 'I will go ahead, warn them there is a riot, that my stock is fleeing this way. I pass the gates often, they know me. Hold here, I will return...'

Anne slowed as Peter galloped and turned a corner.

The street grew quiet. I drew Dill closer. She gripped me back.

'Come on, Peter,' whispered Anne. Far away came the cries of the crowd.

'Evey, where will we go?' Dill's voice was scratched by the noose. 'He will follow. I know he will, Evey.'

'Shush! I knows it, Dill!' I stopped. That was wrong. I wiped dirt from her cheek. 'Don't you worry, I will find us a place. We will be free of him. Just you see.'

She nodded, as she bent her head to my hands. And I fought the ache in my throat, for I did not know where I would go, or what I would do. Only that we must run, as far and as fast as we could.

I heard a horse, its hooves echoed about us, like it rode the very walls. Was this soldiers coming? I hefted my blade, ready.

Peter flew towards us, Shadow flecked with foam.

'Come! Come quickly!'

From back down the street, came shouts and croaks. My kin would nest them all.

Anne kicked, and with Peter beside us, we turned that last corner, and saw the city gates there waiting. Guardsmen held them open to the road beyond.

'Hurry, now! I have told them a stampede is on our tail!'

We charged, pushed and urged those horses to go ever faster.

'God save you, sirs!' Peter called out to those watching guards. 'The herd is frenzied by dogs! Be away from here! Save yourselves!'

And they stepped back to see us pass, our mighty parade.

Dill, all bare legs and tattered dress.

Anne daubed all gold and white.

Peter surging ahead.

And me, my bright blade aloft.

'Yes, make way!' I laughed to see their mouths agape. 'Make way, for this is our day and will be ever more! This fine and glorious day of the witches!'

Then from town, at last, we were free.

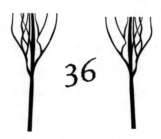

36

'This way, Anne!'

Tracks led every way, churned by wheels and hooves, yet Peter rode where the land grew higher, rising to a steep hill. As we climbed, I breathed the green sweetness, smelled earth and cow and rain.

'They will be watching the roads. Better we head there!'

I followed Peter's finger, ever inky and wise, to the brow of the hill where sat a crown of trees. And something stirred in me then, a memory woken.

'Evey! Pass me the child, you will go faster!'

'I ain't no child. I'm Dill!'

Peter laughed, as she swung to his reaching arm.

'And I'm Peter, and I beg your eternal forgiveness!'

Safe in his arms, she grinned. Dill and Peter, the fastest friends.

'Hold tight, Dilly Doe!'

'I will, Evey Bird!'

Once there was an Evey who would scorn her sister to hear that sing-song name. But then I saw it true, like all her gifts from the woods. It was a name she had found for me, and only me, and I was proud and pleased to hear it.

'We can make it.' Peter spurred on. 'Then I will lead you after dark!'

The hill grew steeper, and we grew slower.

'Do you see them, young Dill?'

'It's just Dill.' She leaned out. 'Not yet! Those crows have been so wily!'

I looked again to the trees, a crown of wood upon a green king. It was like I returned to somewhere I knew but had never been. I shivered for it.

'Evey, what's the matter?' Anne's voice stroked my aching bones. 'Are you ailed?'

'Nay, there's no helping what we have, Greeneye.'

I sensed her smile in her cold grip. 'Then we can only help each other.'

'Quickly, now!' Peter dropped to his feet. 'Into the cover!'

'They're alder, Evey!' Dill skipped to the waiting shade. 'Like our wood back home…'

Our wood. Where we hunted with Mother and hid to watch her die. Seemed we had run so far yet stepped only from our door. I touched the trees, feeling the wind press those bodies.

'Anne, bring the horses, they must not be seen! But we may see them...'

Dill hummed as she plucked leaves, smelling them with a smile. I put the stone in my pocket, but it stayed heavy on my thoughts.

'Dill, my clever mite.' Closely she watched Anne and Peter. 'You know so much. What is the stone doing?'

Then she was gone, running to him. 'What is that there you hold?'

He had a short cane, it was raised to his eye.

'Evey! Come!' Anne motioned to me.

'It is a spyglass.' Peter kneeled by Dill. 'See, look through here...'

Dill raised the stick to her eye, then gave a startled shout.

'I can see for miles! So close! I can see everythin—' She gasped again. 'Riders!'

I didn't need no spy stick to see what she saw. Far below town lay, and as I watched, from its gates flew men on horses. Tall One was coming.

Peter took back his glass. 'Excellent! Jacobs is sending men along the roads. We'll hide here till night, then... Wait... There's a woman. The one from the trial, she's... she's pointing this way.'

I looked to Anne. She didn't need no spyglass neither.

'It's Grey, Evey.' Dill prised the glass from Peter.

'Yes, Dilly. It is.' I drew my blade, as Anne lifted hers.

'There is another way.' Peter looked to us both, thoughts alight. 'They know we're on two horses. And they won't have spyglasses. If we spring from here along the ridge, this Grey will see the horses and think we've fled. And I've got an idea where we can lead them.'

'Or you could flee, Peter Merchantman,' I said. 'For Jessica. And for Fay.'

His eyebrow raised. 'Do you know who my daughter wants to be, when she grows up?'

His smile became Fay's. I saw her chasing apples, putting on her play, dressing me up.

'Tall One's shouting to Grey.' Dill turned from the glass. 'But she won't let up pointin'.'

'This is for her as much for you, Evey. For her future. All the futures of little women like Fay.'

And then Anne was there with the horses. 'Let us go, cousin.'

'No, Anne.'

'Evey, I will find you.' Her eyes were green jewels.

'Take care of my spyglass, Dill!' Peter rose to Shadow. 'I shall return for it!'

With a gentle pull, for I could not stop her, nor never want to, Anne was upon Coal, and he was trotting through the trees.

'And I for you, my friend!' she cried.

I watched their horses leap from the wood, and drive across the hillside. Anne shouted to Peter, their heads bent to the wind. They were full of life, children again.

'Evey, Tall One's chasing now.'

I moved to Dill's side, that spyglass pressed to her eye. We saw those riders split and scurry, give chase to my friend and her cousin. I could hear their hot shouts. It was working. Clever Peter Merchantman.

Dill dropped the glass, as though it scalded her hands.

'Dill?'

She shook her head.

'What? What do you see?'

I picked up that strange stick. A little hole at its end. I brought it to my eye.

It was like I had flown sudden, down that hill and landed among them.

I saw Tall One's face so close, urging his riders to follow.

But. Where was…? I flew along.

There.

Grey hair whipping the wind.

She shouted, and shook her head, pointing up.

Back I flew to Tall One.

He bellowed. He raged. This witch was not listening.

I felt my other hand creep, feeling for the stone. It was warm. Waiting.

'Evey, what are you doing? What's happening?'

I watched as Tall One shouted to the two horsemen. They rode on.

Watched as he pulled his reins over, and veered round.

'Evey, please…'

'They're coming!' I rounded on her. 'Peter's plan didn't work and they're coming!'

The stone shook in my grip.

'Evey, please don't—'

'Shush it, Dill!'

I didn't care. I cared only to fly down that glass, down that hill, to find her.

I saw Tall One charging, his horse mad-eyed, champing at the bit.

I swung the glass, too fast across her smile. I moved back. Found her.

'Evey…'

Grey was so far from me, but she looked straight, right at the woods, right at me.

'Evey, please put down the stone.'

And my hand was shaking so much it hurt.

'Evey!'

I would kill her. The stone had made me so strong.

'Evey, let go now!'

I would throttle the smile from her.

I felt the spyglass move in my grip. Like a... Fast I took it from my eye.

A snake writhed in my fingers. It hissed, jaws opening.

Tearing in my hand. I was bitten. And the stone fell.

I cried out and hurled that snake away.

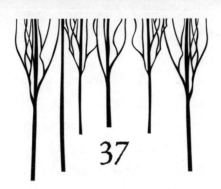

37

'Dill!' I fell into her. 'Quickly, the snake.'

'There ain't no snake, Evey.'

'There is, look…'

But only the spyglass was on the ground. No serpent of black and—

Grey.

I looked down to see her far below, still standing, still watching, as Tall One hollered ahead, like he was her pup, and she the proud parent.

'It was her, weren't it? Casting a spell through that stick?'

'No, it weren't.' Dill picked up the glass. 'It was you.'

'Me?' I turned to her.

'It's why I had to bite you. I am sorry, Evey…' She hopped up, a little redbreast among the trees. 'You were holding it. And you were thinking about her.' She waved the stone, glinting in the shade.

'I thought that was...' I felt those fangs pressing, piercing. 'It was so real, Dill.'

'The stone is powerful.' She took my hand, thin fingers pulling at mine. 'And you are so strong, Evey Bird. It's why Mother gave it me till you were ready. Come, now, I will help you.'

She put her arm about me, while I stumbled for understanding.

'But, Dilly... Mother gave you her stone because you are so gifted... you know things I could never... you're like Mother. I'm not like you...'

The words did not fit right in my mouth no more. I felt my cheeks grow hot with saying them. They made me sound like a silly jealous child. And I knew more than ever that I had left that child far behind.

'Silly Evey Bird.' Dill pushed back her black nest. It was like she heard that word in my mind, but she was so gentle, not teasing.

'Mother gave me the stone to keep safe for you.'

She reached to stroke my cheek.

'For you are more magick than all of us. You didn't know it or want to know it.'

I stared at her, as the shouts rose, as the wind blustered, as I stood amid the shame of my memories. What I had thought, and harboured so long against her and Mother, was shedding from me like the skin of a toad.

'Keep it safe? What do you mean, Dill?'

She pulled at each my fingers, counting them over, like when she was a kit.

'Till you understood the stone better, Evey. Mother told me to help you. But you were too angry with her... and with me.' She smiled, a flash of teeth under her billowing hair, then she frowned.

'And the stone is so dangerous, Evey, if you...'

'If you what, Dilly?'

Dill turned my hand and traced the cuts there.

'The stone is our protection, Evey. We must do good things, always, to keep it so.'

I thought of it in my fist, a shield against a falling blade. Her fingers smoothed mine.

'Your anger brought those crows. But it couldn't stop them.'

I thought of Mother's healing way. I thought of Dill's care for creatures.

'Even if we fight, Evey, like you fight so well,' her fingers tugged at my thoughts, 'we must do it with good in us.'

I looked to her, and from far above, I heard the low growl of thunder. Like Grey, dripping her poison to the fear that hid in my heart.

Feed it your anger.

'Dilly, Grey tricked me. She told me things...'

But Dill turned and tugged the harder, urging me into those moaning trees.

'Most likely!' she shouted over her shoulder. 'She's a wicked witch, ain't she? Come on, now...'

'I think Grey wants the stone.' I stopped her to listen. 'But if she does, why didn't she take it from me at the coven?'

Dill looked down to the stone in her hand, then back to me.

'Mother always said the stone should be given or found, never taken, Evey.'

She hopped, itching to be among the smells of root and earth.

'But... I took it... from you, that night.'

'I knows it.' She swung my hand. 'It's why I fretted for you so.' Then she shrugged off her frown, and jumped on, bright as anything.

'But it's back now and so are you. Hurry up! You are such a slow snail!'

And she was away into the wood, her words rustling in the leaves.

Given or found, never taken.

I heard a cry behind us, and the hairs upon my neck prickled.

It was a hero's bellow, for only heroes hunt young witches.

The wind whistled, made those tall trees thresh.

I smelled rabbit. A burrow of babes sleeping deep. Sudden I wanted to dig down and disappear, but I buried my worry instead.

'You're not going to hide, are you, Evey?'

She lifted the truth from my heart, as easy as she moved the stone in her palms.

'I am not, Dilly. But I will lift you into—'

'I ain't hiding neither.'

She looked me straight and sure.

'Dill—'

'No, Evey, I ain't sitting in no tree waitin' to be picked. We hunt together,' she said. 'It's the only way.'

I saw how fierce she was, her fury at what they had taken from us, this so-called hunter, this so-called witch, this dog, this bitch.

And as I heard the creak of saddle, the rattle of reins, I brought my little sister close, and breathed in her body, as both we remembered what we had run from, what we would run from no more.

'Witches! I know you're in there, witches!'

We crouched to watch him, our hunter.

'I will flush you out, like the vermin you are!'

Tall One dropped from his horse, and slow drew his gun.

'Grey ain't with him, Evey…'

I watched that dog sniff for us.

'She's slid away. It's what snakes do.'

She grinned. We were together, in our woods again.

His shape moved across the yellow light, black in the blacker trees.

'I will make him fire aplenty,' Dill said. 'He will waste his powder to catch me.' I felt her stroke my hair, as she readied to go.

'Dill…'

I trembled for her loving touch, and for my worry to keep her safe, to protect her ever always. Though I had sworn to Mother, she was my sister, and I need never swear for that.

'Don't worry, my Evey Bird.' Her eyes glittered, like those stars upon the stone. 'Mother taught us too good. And you are stronger, sister, but I am always faster than you.'

She pressed her fingers to my lips, and I kissed them. How she had grown in these few days. Tall like the alder trees above us. And like them, she would not be pushed.

'Till light be sought, my Dill.'

'Till dogs be dirt, my Evey.'

My promise was her promise.

'We fly for you, Mother,' we whispered both.

My children.

Then we sprang to it. Daughters. Sisters. Witches who love to hunt.

38

The musket cracked. Bark burst to gold splinters. But Dill was gone, a cartwheel of feet and laughter.

'Damn you to hell!'

I saw Tall One bend to chide his smoking gun, as Dill jumped high to touch branches, like she climbed upon the air itself. She was right. She was faster than me.

CRACK!

'Blast you, wild cat!'

'Yes!' Dill laughed and sprang on. 'I am a cat! Raarr!' Her fingers became claws.

I watched them move like paper puppets, the trees their stage, the hunter ever chasing, never catching his quarry, like a deer dancing forever beneath the flame of the sun.

'Child, I will skin you alive if I waste another bullet!'

'Not wasted, Master Jacobs!' Dill cried. 'We are having fun!'

How lithe she was, how her hair flowed, her slender arms sliding among the trunks of those trees, like they were her passing partners under the maypole.

'Careful, Dill… Stay ahead of him, now.'

Above me I heard a sound of rustling. I looked up.

An owl blinked, a white queen awoken.

'This way, Master Jacobs!' Dill called. 'This way!'

We had him in our embrace, my sister and me.

'Devil take you, child!' Tall One fumbled for his powder.

'This way, Dilly… This way…'

For the hunter was hunted, and I heard the fear that rose in his voice, ringing in that wood, that home of our hearts, where we would bring balance for the wrong he did.

Closer, closer I watched him come.

Till silent I sprang, soft earth and seeds and leaves under my toes, and I saw his comely face now a sheen of sweat.

'I will kill you both! Like I killed your mother!'

A shriek behind me. The white queen flew. Dill danced on.

'I see you!'

A flurry of wings. He raised his arms.

'Bloody birds! Get away!'

And in her wake, I flew too.

'Mother!' Dill cried.

'Yes.' And lifted my sword. 'For Mother.'

'Mother! It's you!'

I turned.

And I saw who Dill saw there at the edge of the woods. A woman. I saw her long hair flowing black against the eye of the sun.

Mother.

Who kneeled and opened her arms to Dill.

And cried out to her daughter in a voice that made me ache.

'My Dilly Dee! Come to me!'

So that Dill ran laughing towards her.

'Mother!'

'Come! My Dill, oh, my Dilly Doe!'

'The stone brought you! I knew it would!'

'Oh, it did, my Dilly Dear! It did!'

And my heart drummed, as I began to run, for Tall One spied Dill leaping through the light. And the hunter was raising his gun...

'DILL!'

I ran. I ran. This could not be.

'Mother!'
Her laughter filled the wood, made it blossom with joy.

Sunlight on steel, turning, clicking.

'Run to me!'
She was not Mother, could not be Mother, for Mother was dead. Mother was dead.

'Come… little Dill!'
Dill stopped. Her smile dropped. That name she hated.

Tall One fired.

But Dill did not spin away. Like a cartwheel. Like a dancing deer.

She fell.

And Grey turned her face to the dying light.
And smiled.

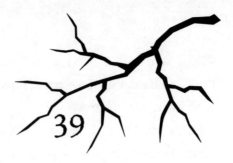

39

'D-Dill!'
    I could not see her, roots caught my feet, as faster, faster I ran.

'Dill…!'

I cried out, tore leaves away, because I could not see her. I could not see—

She lay beneath a tree.

'Dill! Please, no…'

I fell to her side. She whimpered, blood on her chest, her fist. So black in the light. No.

'NO!'

I pressed to her chest, my fingers slipping. This could not be.

'Dilly, nonono.'

I smoothed her hair, pushed blood across her brow. She groaned.

'Dill? My Dill?'

She stirred, her eyes flickered.

'Ev… Ev…'

'Dilly, hold still…'

I pressed harder, had to stop it flowing.

'Ah! Evey, it… it hurts!'

'I know, my Dilly… I know… shush…'

'Evey, I'm sorry.'

Her fingers gripped to my arm, sticky.

'I so… so wanted it to be… Mother, I'm s-stupid…'

'Shush, now.' I felt for her wound. 'I'm the stupid one, remember?' Clutching at her.

'But, Evey… the stone…'

She opened her bloody fist. The stone was split in two.

'It flew against me when…'

I stroked her blood away, to see only a bruise upon her chest. Yet she was not hit.

'The stone cut me when he… he fired.'

There was a deep gash across her shaking palm, yet she was alive. She was alive.

'It saved you, Dill!' I choked tears and held her ashen face.

'You were right, Mary Tell!'

I turned. A tall shape far across the wood, astride the sun. Dill tried to stand.

'Shh.' I pressed her back, a finger to her lips. 'Lie still for me.' I wrapped my arms about her, pulled her shuddering body to the shadows, as I watched Tall One stop and curse, and cast his musket aside.

'That wild cat was hard to hit, and now my powder is gone! But I need no gun...'

He drew his sword, scraping the dusk. He was coming, had to hurry. I tore a strip from my dress and bound it tight to Dill's hand.

'Dill, you must rest.' I folded her fingers over the binding.

'No... Evey, we must fight together...'

'Quickly, man!' Grey shouted. 'One more remains...'

'I can count, woman.'

'Evey, he's coming...'

The wind keened and I knew then what we must do. Like this wailing wood, this strange crown of trees, was waiting for me to know, had been waiting always.

I drew Dill to me. 'They think you're dead, Dill. So, shall we play a game?'

She stopped her pushing to me and smiled at that.

I stroked her shaking arm. 'For our game, will you promise to stay hidden, my Dilly Doe?'

Her eyes lit to hear me say that, Mother's sing-song name.

'I promise, Evey Bird.'

I turned from my sister, and as I stole through the trees, I thought of all Tall One had done to my family, to the young, the old, the innocent.

So I ran to him then, like lost lovers all met.

'I shall enjoy this, girl.'

'I'm no girl,' I said, for I knew what I was at last, 'I am Eveline of the Birds.'

He laughed. 'Well, my red robin,' and he swiped his sword, 'time to clip those wings!'

He came for me. Swinging like a hero.

I breathed out and jumped away.

His noble blade bit to a tree that held it, and I circled.

'By God, I'll...'

He pulled, but I lunged the quicker, and swung him full away. Away from Dill.

Drunk with lust, he tipped to his knees, pawing for balance. He grinned then, dirt across his swarthy cheek.

'You are nimble, my little bird...'

I wanted to smash his lovely teeth down his lovely throat.

'You could have helped in the war,' he pulled his blade free, 'instead of dying here.'

'I don't help dogs.' I stepped before him. 'I hunt them.'

Snarling, he pounced, but I sprang high upon a fallen tree, rotted wood underfoot, beetles crushing. I would crush him.

'You witch kind!' he barked. 'You're nothing!'

It was time to draw the truth.

'Yet, didn't we witches win your war?' I shouted. 'Help you rout the king?'

And I remembered the dying words of an old woman, howling for her love, lost to us but never forgotten. Not never, Tess. I swear.

'Isn't that why *she* lives…?'

I thrust my blade towards Grey, that watching, smiling snake.

'Why you both hunted our kind? To hide your bloody pact?'

The wind caught my fury, whirling my words.

'Why you killed my mother?'

I flew at him, swinging wild, slicing the light.

'Answer me! Answer me!'

Our blades kissed hard and I tripped, tumbling to the earth.

Down he drove, his steel hissing my name.

I rolled as it stuck the empty ground.

Again he hacked. Again I rolled, his blade licking my hand. I kicked, rolling, rolling over. And as I did, I felt the grip of my sword move. Peter's hidden blade.

'Tell me the truth!' I breathed, as his smitten maid. 'Before you kill me, sir…'

Tall One held to savour the sight of me, my chest heaving with battle, ready for him. And as raindrops pattered the leaves, he looked to me and yet not to me.

'I told them,' his eyes marked Grey, and he sneered, 'never trust a witch, and yet here I am, at the end of the world, with two of you.'

'Them?' My hand crept along the handle. 'Who do you speak of?'

His eyes, hard as flint, came back to mine,

'Powerful men, child. For I am just a foot soldier. Doing God's work.'

'What are you waiting for? Finish her, Jacobs!'

He scowled at Grey spoiling our tryst.

'But one day, they shall know my name...' Slow he raised his sword. 'And what is truth, little bird? Once I have nested you...'

The handle turned in my fingers, and Peter's voice came whispering on the wind.

Two blades lie slumbering...

Tall One winked only for me. Peter's quick eye darted so clever.

'...Then this pact with her will be over...'

Turn back to loose the daughter...

'...And I will kill this Mary Tell,' he growled in the shadow. 'And you will all be dead with your truth!'

I twisted my hand, back. The knife hatched.

'For truth is the story we make, girl...' His voice swelled, like he roused his beloved crowd. But only I was there to watch his great show. 'And it is men like me who will make the story of this land, you hear? Men like me!'

Only I was there, to see how tall he grew, tall as the trees, tall as the billowing sky.

'Not you! You damn...' he cried so mighty, so strong, 'witch!'

He swung. I flung.

And I watched my knife fly, brighter than his dull blade.

...*who is swift and deadly.*

I watched this man, this story, fall to his knees, like he prayed one last to his god.

I watched him weep, tears of running red, as he raised his arm, like I first saw him, raising it high, as to hail me. And I knew then, as sure as Mother's life that he took that day, I had scryed this. For he hailed not me, but Death, who waited at my shoulder.

Then Tall One fell down, dead. As a dog.

Shaking to stand, I looked to him, now but a body, not a hero, not a killer, and I could not stem the tears, for all that had been, all that was done by him, and done by me.

'You did it! My little weapon! You did it!'

Grey's laugh, a dagger across my skin.

'The stone has made you strong!'

She had played us all.

'You fed it so well, Evey!'

But our game was not finished.

'My sister!' I shouted. 'My sister is dead!'

And stumbled through the trees, thunder at my heels.

'Yes! And the stone is turning, Evey! You clever girl!'

But my sister was not dead. She looked to me from the shadow, as I sobbed, and she smiled such a smile, full of life and light.

'Ah, Evey, do not mourn for long. We have family matters.'

Grey raised her arms to the sky and sang,

'*There was a valley…*'

Her fingers became a fist that pulled, as if she roped the wind itself.

'*And in that valley…*'

With a grunt, she flung towards a hill far beyond the town.

'*Was a woman…*'

And we felt hissing heat as the sky cracked, and down roared a spear of white fire.

'*…of witching way.*'

Then we watched that hill burn.

'Evey.' Dill's hand was cold and wet. 'Mother said the stone should only be given and found.' Her eyes shone with knowing. 'What if taking the stone makes it go bad? Makes you strong, but wrong…'

She turned the pieces in her hands, as the thunder rolled.

Grey hurled again, and again it came at her bidding, a spike that split the clouds and torched the earth. She had such power. Such awful power.

'Evey, listen. When you took the stone from me, I think it started to turn.'

I looked to my sister, remembering Grey's words.

Give the stone all your anger, and it will make you strong.

'But I took the stone from you, Dill.' Shame welled in me. 'And I was strong, I felt it... I felt it all.'

I thought of Meakin, I thought of the crows, of Tall One, such anger riding me.

'And things... things are wrong... Our friends are gone, you are hurt and now the stone is broken...'

Doubt and fear filled the dark around me. What was I doing? I couldn't do this.

Grey coiled the air about her fists.

I felt Dill press a shard of the stone to my hand.

'We are not broken, Evey.' She closed my fingers around it. Once smooth and round, now the stone was sharp and jagged.

'Grey says the stone is turning, Evey.' Her teeth bared in the shadow, like the clever fox she had always been, always would be. 'I say not. Not with the good in us.'

Lightning lit her cunning smile.

I stroked the edge of the broken stone, and I thought on a time long past with Mother, when we sheltered from a storm, and she held to us, soothed us, told us to count.

'One...'

And Dill smiled the wider, remembering same.

'Two...' she whispered as Mother whispered.

'Three...'

The thunder bellowed, tried to frighten us. But we would not be afeared. Not never.

'Dilly, will you keep counting? And come when I call?'

'I will, Evey.'

She lifted her piece of stone to one eye, winked with the other.

'Then shall we make magick, Dill? You and I?'

She grinned, like the light came from her, not the sky.

'Evvvvvveeeyyyy.'

My hairs prickled. Mother calling me in. But it was not Mother.

'Come to meeeeee...'

I watched Dill unwind her binding, and I saw her turn that stone shard through her wound, made it wet in the flickering light. So I drew back the dressing, and pressed my stone, opening the wound. It hurt, but how good it felt to make this with my sister.

'Evey! You have wept long enough! Come!'

She threw. Lightning drove into the hill, shaking the trees.

I held the shard in my bloody palm. Dill closed hers upon mine, joining our hands. This was our spell and we knew the words. They were carved on our hearts that day she left us.

'For my sister's blood,' I said.

'For your blood,' Dill said.

'For Mother's blood,' we said.

'Evey! Bring me that stone! Or I will burn your burrow to cinders!'

Grey turned to face our wood, and the clouds gathered.

I stood. Dill nodded.

'I will come, Evey. When you call.'

The sky lit, and she began to count,

'One...'

I kissed the stone. Grey told me once that it was not for little girls. I ran from my sister then, to find our aunt, and show her we weren't girls no more.

We were witches. And she would know it.

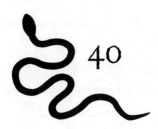

40

'Welcome, Eveline of the Birds!'

I stepped beyond the trees to face her.

'Your mother hated my storm riding!'

The thunder laughed with Grey.

'Oh, but, Evey, she would be so proud of you. All those men slain... calling those crows... And now you have killed Jacobs for me!' She bowed. 'All you, Evey! Beautiful. Angry. You!'

'You tricked me!'

I raised the stone, saw the flicker of desire in her eyes.

'No, Evey. I told you the truth. What your mother would not.'

We circled same, a mirror of witches.

'She was too stuck in her fool ways. The war of men has changed this land.'

'She weren't a fool!'

'And now her stone is turning, Evey. You have seen to that.'

'No!' I felt that cold hardening of anger. I must fight it. To fight her.

We must do good things, always.

I gritted my teeth, as I kept the stone high.

'It cannot be taken! You know that!'

Grey watched my arm shake.

'When our mother gave the stone to my sister, I was so jealous, Evey.' Her eyes narrowed against the silver rain. 'Just like you.'

'I'm not like you! I'll never give you the stone!'

She frowned then, and in her face I saw a jealous child, who wanted what she could not have. She raised her arms.

'Very well, Eveline…'

Became a blur, sliding away quick.

'If you will not give it, and I cannot take it…'

I swung. Missed. And all became bright as a summer's morn.

'Then I will find it…'

Her fingers wrenched the clouds.

'Beside your dead body!'

And she hurled. Lightning lashed, whipping white.

The wood shrieked to flame.

Dill!

I fell, the wind snatching away my blade.

Pain scored my skull, sound snuffed. And Grey circled me, smiling, ever smiling.

One...

Still I gripped the stone.

Two...

Thunder roared and rocked.

I looked to the trees. There against the flames, I saw her.

'Dill,' I whispered, aching to stand. 'Not yet.'

'You're right, Evey...' Grey stepped before me. 'Not like me. Like your mother.'

I was not afeared of her. I was not. I was not.

'Your heart is good. You want to give. That's how your mother saw the stone. To cure, to scry and soothe.' She sighed. 'So boring...'

Her shining eyes upon me.

'Mother.' Pain burning, biting my side. 'Help me...'

I felt the heat. Felt Dill watching.

'Jacobs was right. The time of the witches is over... Now it is the time of men, to forge this land anew.'

She turned to gaze upon town, its firefly lights, its smoking dreams.

'Men who love their wars, who will kill their king. And need a new queen!'

The wind dropped, and light coursed the clouds.

'And your queen demands a weapon. A powerful weapon...'

She lifted her hands. I ran at her.

'...of stone!'

The hill turned white.

One...

Fire crashed. I rolled, coughing, gasping.

Grey stalked through the wind and the rain.

'You have battled well, little bird, but you are too tired, too weak.'

She looked towards the fire.

'And you are just another fool, another dead witch—'

She saw something, behind me.

'It cannot be!'

I turned. Two shapes now against the flames.

Their hands reached for mine.

'Now, Dill! Come to me!'

'No!' Grey cried. 'You are both dead!'

As Mother watched us from that wood of my dreams. As her daughter, my sister, came to me, fast as a cat, her face so happy. And we turned and looked upon Grey, her hair snaking, her fingers curled to the storm.

'You are all dead!'

Then together we ran.

Down the hill, leaving our pain behind.

We lifted our hands that held our stone, our beating heart, as we leaped, and cried, 'For our blood!'

Let fly, two black birds swift and true, where Grey screamed to see them come.

And knew she was dead.

As the stones struck her head, and her hands dropped, and light hit the wood, the hill, all the world around, and we fell back.

Into Mother's arms.

41

I dreamed of Dill as a babe. She was crying.

I opened my eyes to see two birds, chirping through a sky as pink as her cheeks. Mother had laid her soft to my arms, that milky weight of her. How quick she stopped her holler. How dark her watching eyes, black seeds shining for me.

'What are they, Evey? You know the birds...'

They called and swooped through the setting sun.

'Swifts. See their curved wing, the tail.'

'They're so fast!'

I pinched her nose. 'Even faster than you, little mite.'

She squealed and rolled to stand. 'Oh, Evey... look, those poor trees...'

I stood slow, my head pounding, and I saw the smoke that drifted from the wood so bent and broken.

'Come on...'

I took her hand, and the swifts followed as we moved through those still bodies full of heat, feeling buried fire beneath our feet.

And we found him at last, lying where I left him.

'From ash we rise, Dill...'

Tall One. The hunter hunted.

'To ash we go, Evey.' She swung my hand.

'Evey!'

We both heard it with a start.

A voice I knew so well.

'Evey!'

And we were running back, coughing smoke, kicking ash to get to her.

As through the smoke, my friend came.

'I found you!'

And Anne was dropping her reins and hugging me. Her cold hands feeling my face. Feeling I was alive.

'Are you hurt?' She looked to us.

'Only that you left me, Anne Greeneye,' I laughed, as Peter watched with the horses.

'Peter Merchantman!' Dill jumped to him. 'I have your spyglass safe!'

'A miracle, Dill.' He looked about to that ravaged place. 'Keep it.'

She grinned so wide, and tears of joy choked me.

'Is that...?'

I blinked where Anne pointed on the hill. The wind lifted the smoke, like a drape to hide dark things.

'Another dead witch. Yes.' I drew my friend away.

'Those riders chased you…' Dill peered through her glass to Peter.

'Aye, Cap'n!' Peter squinted. 'And were sunk easy in that savage storm, so they were!' He doffed his sailor's cap and Dill giggled for more.

'Evey…' Anne pointed. 'Your stone.'

It lay on the grass. I remembered how it spun swift and sure from my fingers.

'I thought it was black…?'

It had been, but now it was white as lightning from a dark storm. As the smile of my sister, whose hand found mine, a mouse back to its burrow.

'It's whole again… That's good, ain't it, Evey?'

'Yes, that's good.' I stroked the hair from her mouth. 'Shall we find it together, Dill?'

Her eyes shone, and she nodded.

So we reached down, and our fingers found it, and lifted the stone.

'Ooh, it's hot, Evey!'

I laughed to watch her, swinging our hands that held all we had of Mother, her warm heart. Mother who was not there. Mother who could not—

And I was on my knees, crying so hard.

'Evey...'

'Balance is got, Dill. But she will not see us now... Mother will never see us...'

'Oh, Evey Bird...'

'Not never again.'

I grabbed to Dill and to Anne, and their arms circled me tight, and I felt Peter's hand upon my hair, as I sobbed, as those swifts cried over me, with me, through me.

'Evey.' Anne's smile trembled. 'My sister is here...' Her hand upon her chest.

'Just as your mother is...' And she pressed my aching heart.

I shivered and looked beyond the trees, back to a land that held no home for us.

'Evey, come.' Dill urged me to rise. 'Come with me.'

Then pulling me on, ever pulling me on, she made around the smouldering woods, to where the wind blew softer, and the sun was falling into the land that ran away to a glittering sea.

'Shh... there in their beating hearts...' Dill pointed down the hill.

A rabbit and her kits, their white tails leaping away.

She pointed to the grass, bending in the breeze.

'See there, how it moves...'

She cupped her hand to the orange light.

'And here, in the sun that warms you...'

Then Dill squinted to me through that black nest of hair.

'She is everywhere.'

And pressed the stone in our hands, so warm and safe between us.

'Wherever we go, she is with us, and she sees us,' she said, then frowned. 'So I do not want you a sad sister, Evey. And Mother would not want that neither.'

She waggled her finger, a little Mother in her way. Little mite always right. I smiled to see her serious, as she lifted her spyglass.

'Across the water, there is a place full of magick, Evey. Mother's old land...'

I looked out to the sea. Looked back, a long time.

'Can we go there, Evey?' Dill leaned her head to my wounded side, and it ached, but I cared not, because she was with me now and forever more. 'Can we go to the island of Air?'

'Eire!' I laughed.

'Eeirre!' she shrieked with glee.

Then I kneeled and drew her in. 'Dill, will you teach me? About the stone? About magick? Everything that Mother taught you?'

Those black eyes shone and she slipped her arm through mine.

'I will. If you will teach me how to hunt and fight. Everything that Mother taught you.'

Anne whistled for Coal, who snorted, ready to run. And a hand all inky, pressed Shadow's reins to mine. Peter Merchantman smiled, then bowed to Dill.

'Take care of your sister.' He shook her hand.

'Aye, Cap'n!' She winked his sailor's wink.

'Well, Eveline of the Birds,' smiled my green-eyed friend. 'Shall we go?'

I breathed the smell of the sodden earth, the salt from the sea.

Mother's land. Full of magick.

'Yes.' And I pointed to the beckoning blue. 'Let us go.'

'Ah, Evey! You are the best sister!' laughed my Dill. 'The very best I know!'

Then we followed her into the sun, dancers all of the day.

Author's Note and Acknowledgements

From his first 'investigation' into the accused, tried and executed Elizabeth Clarke — a scared old woman (who had only one leg, which meant she had to be helped up the gallows' steps) — the self-titled Witchfinder General, Matthew Hopkins, blazed a bloody trail across the East of England blighted by the first English Civil War.

Between 1645 to 1647, Hopkins and his keen collaborator, John Stearne, were particularly adept in their drive to root out witches, travelling the length of the county to extract testimony from eager witnesses.

For while the Witchfinders were powered by puritanical zeal, they did not act alone – a witch hunt needs its accusers, its storytellers, its crowd. With the country divided and terrified, the war was the perfect breeding ground for suspicion and blame.

Witch hunts still happen. Wars have not stopped. Abuse is alive and well. Racism refuses to quit. History should be about learning from our mistakes, building towards a better future, although it seems power remains a sweet craving for the human race. But we must believe in the next generation, and the one after that, and the next, that they will simply lose the taste for such things, and pass on the truth of what happened, what must not happen again.

Evey and Dill are from the seventeenth century, but their sibling nature is for any time. Even in the darkest moments, like them we can still delight in a new day, dance and name the birds. Even if our brother or sister has driven us into a rage, under it all, they are our kin. There is no one who knows our hearts and dreams better, and their fierce love is what makes life worth fighting for.

Over the course of researching this book, I have been indebted to several excellent historical studies:

Diane Purkiss' invaluable *The English Civil War: A people's history*; Malcolm Gaskill's enlightening and gruesome *Witchfinders: A seventeen century English tragedy*; David and Andrew Pickering's comprehensive catalogue of the trials, *Witch Hunt: The persecution of Witches in England*; John Wroughton's absorbing in-depth social studies, *An Unhappy Civil War: The experiences of ordinary people in Gloucestershire, Somerset and Wiltshire 1642-1646*, and *A community at war: The Civil War in Bath and North Somerset*; Blare Worden's ever handy and concise, *The English Civil Wars 1640-1660*; and Christopher Hill's epic of political, religious and philosophical fervour, *A World Turned Upside Down: Radical ideas during the English Revolution*.

I am also thankful, to the utmost, to all those people who have helped bring this book into being. My parents, Jacqui and Colin. My sister, Sally. My wife, Abby, my children, Molly and Sam, and her furriness, Coco. The writing fraternity at Bath Spa, in particular my workshop gang: Anna Morgan, Maddy Woosnam, Kirsty Applebaum,

Christina Wheeler, Julie Pike, Imogen Dyckhoff, Anna Hoghton, Helen Lipscombe, Zoe Cookson, Beatrice Wallbank, Mark Rutherford, Laura Kadner, Paul Veart, Dandy Smith, Sue Birrer, Sarah House, Kathryn Clark, and to the memory of Jacqui Catcheside and her huge smile. My tutors, Steve Voake for his encouragement and warmth for the first spark of this story; Lucy Christopher for a life-changing Arvon, her beady eye and boundless energy; Julia Green for being the heart and soul of writing for children. Janine Amos for her wisdom and enthusiasm. David Almond for pure inspiration. My sparring partner, Chris Vick, for absolutely everything and more, thank you, sir. All my colleagues at Aardman who have cheered me on over the years, in particular Dan Efergan and Lorna Probert for their unstinting support and help. My agent, Catherine Pellegrino, for her intelligence, patience and having the best name and laugh in the known universe. My publisher and editor, Fiona Kennedy, for her unbridled passion for Evey and Dill, thank you so much. The collective might at Zephyr: Lauren Atherton, Clémence Jacquinet, Jessie Price, Ben Prior, Jade Gwilliam, Jessie Sullivan. Anthony Cheetham for founding such an awesome publishing house in Head of

Zeus. Laura Smythe for her publicity nous. And the god of book covers that is Edward Bettison.

By the time they were done, the witchfinders of the 1640s had brought some three hundred men and women to trial, and more than a hundred of these had lost their lives. No one knows the precise number.

So, in closing, this book is finally in memory of all those people, the lost, the ones we should never forget.

Finbar Hawkins
Wiltshire
July 2020

Read the first chapter of

Finbar Hawkins' new book,

STONE

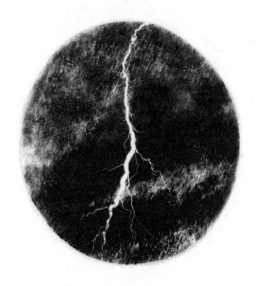

Coming in September 2022

Dad went to the desert one day and never came back.

He was killed as he was driving his squad through the centre of Kabul. It was a routine morning thing, they were passing through a busy market, when the suicide bomber struck.

A car packed with explosives rammed their truck, killing them all.

Ten civilians also lost their lives.

The suicide bomber was seventeen. My age.

And tomorrow we bury Dad.

My dad, who went to that desert, who never said goodbye to me.

I

Chad said there was a party at Darren's, his folks were off. Spot on. That's what I needed. Mum wasn't pleased.

'It's your dad's funeral in the morning, Sam.'

'Exactly, Mum,' I say, as I pull on my jacket. 'Why do you think I'm going?'

There are girls dancing in a darkened room. Lads watching from the bright kitchen. Timbo, Sharkey and Ben and some younger kid I don't know. They've got ciders on the go. I swipe one, expecting them to grab it back, but nobody's bothered, too merry on the *thrum thrum thrum* of that dark room.

There's Rache, and Tash by her side, as always. And May, and moody Gina. They're laughing and swaying to some grime track, and then I see this girl I've not seen before.

'Now, who's that?' says Chad.

Sharkey doesn't turn, flicking his long hair over his can.

'Oona something,' he slurs. 'Family's just arrived from barracks in Germany.'

I swig on the cider, feeling the sour tang hit my belly. Don't really like booze, but then I don't want to stand out. I can feel the younger kid's eyes on me.

'Is there a sign above my head or something?'

'What?'

'Does it say 'Dead Dad' above my head?'

'No...' He flushes, looking around at the others, who look down, bite lips. 'I'm sorry...'

'Sorry for staring, or sorry about my dad?' I swig again, and the kid looks ready to run.

'Sam!' Chad leans across. 'Come dance.'

'No, I don't—'

The girls shriek with laughter. I turn to see they're looking this way. I catch Oona's eye, a black flash.

Then in the dark, on the sofa, I spot Andy Miller, grinning and shouting to the music, raising a muscled arm in the air.

The music changes, *mum-mum-mum, ahhing* off the walls.

The girls cheer and pull the girl called Oona into their dance. I like this song, working its magic on the fire in me. I feel bad for having a go at that boy. I turn back to him. But there's just a can and an empty chair.

'Classic, Sam! Come on!' Chad's pulling me too, and I don't want to, not if they're all watching, but that girl's in there, and I want to get closer to her.

'Whoop! Whoop! Come on!'

I see Rache and Tash swap looks as we enter the dark room. Everyone's here for me, but then nobody knows what to say. But I don't want them to say anything. I just want them to be normal. Then Rache smiles and turns the volume up and we cheer, letting the music fold us in.

The girl with the huge eyes throws shapes, her shadow on the wall. Andy bounces on the sofa, banging his head on the ceiling. Chad's grinning through his dark brows, as he sidles between Rache and Tash, and I'm laughing, at how good it feels, how nothing matters here. But then I find myself standing off and watching the three of them, feel my smile ache. They all crouch, singing together.

I see Oona smiling as she pushes back her long dark hair, and as I watch her, she mouths the words, that everyone shouts,

'Oh, whoa, oh oh,
Oh, oh oh'

Chad has gone into a conga with Rache, spinning

between the girls who are all laughing at him, the clown.

He goes mock serious at Rache, who turns to Tashe and Oona copies him, hands in the air.

The room shakes, as Chad moves towards her, and I'm watching them, dancing closer and closer, and the girls are singing, but now Rache is watching like me.

Over Chad's shoulder, Oona shoots me a look, a dark arrow of eyes that stops me dead. Chad leans in and speaks to her, this girl who smiles at me. She says something back, and Chad can't hear of course, and isn't that funny. She grins, the kitchen light catching the gap in her two front teeth. I love her teeth.

And as the music and bodies move around them, I want to go forward and say something to her, barge Chad out of the way, so I can see her smile at me again.

But Oona laughs as Chad pulls a face, that silly handsome face. And Rache is watching like me, because she's thinking like me, thinking of Chad. We all know she's thinking of Chad.

Oona glances at him, then back at me. She looks down as she dances and it's as if she's in slow motion, freckles spreading across her smile, and she's so beautiful, so very beautiful.

Sharkey knocks into me, shouting.

And as I watch them, I'm frozen to the spot. But I

can't do anything, just watch. I'm stuck. Stuck forever.
Can't do anything.

Chad leaning close to Oona. Her white ear turned
to him.

I can't be here anymore. I shouldn't have come. I
feel sick.

I push Sharkey out of the way, sloshing his cider.

I barge through Chad and Oona, glad to spoil their
fun.

'Sam?'

Chad calls behind me. Rache jumps clear.

'All right! Slow down!'

But I don't, and I don't care as I push past moody
Gina.

Andy Miller sees me coming, slides the doors open.

I ignore his goofy grin as I yank curtains aside, dive
into the dark.

My breath is coming hard.

I throw my hands out, my knuckles catching the
wall, and the pain makes me so angry, that I want to
scream, hit something really hard.

I'm in a little garden, a security light burns my eyes.
Garden stuff everywhere, a plastic sandpit, a chair and
a mauled football. I run two steps and whack it hard
against the wall.

I sit on the chair, breathing, breathing, trying to

catch my breath, thinking how I don't like this song anymore.

Thinking of the girl called Oona I couldn't talk to.

Thinking of my best friend Chad who could.

Thinking, why couldn't I be more like him?

Thinking what Dad would say.

*

'Are you ok?'

Oona is standing by the wall.

'Were you sick?'

'No!'

I can't help it, my voice bursts out, I'm flaming angry at flaming everything.

'I'm sorry… I didn't…'

She moves into the garden, light touching the tips of her hair, and slowly, she sits on edge of the sandpit thing.

'It's okay.'

I look at her now, her face in the glare, and her immense inky eyes swallow me whole. Her skin is so white and clear, and freckles splash across her nose and cheeks. A single dark eyebrow raises under a few falling strands of her hair. And I don't know why, I just want to take her hand, and open the back gate and run away from this party, this town, this place.

'I'm Oona, by the way.'

'I know.'

That eyebrow raises again.

'Little bit stalkery, Sam...'

The laugh jumps out of me.

'Yeah, sorry... I heard... I meant...' She watches me, grinning. 'Someone said...' I can't get my words to behave, all jostling to get out and impress her.

She laughs too and stands, 'It's cold out here. Shall we—'

'No! Not back in there.'

Oona looks down at my hand holding hers. I didn't know I had grabbed it. She takes a step closer, eyes searching me, eyes that see me and only me. My hand trembles. Like my lip.

'You're not ok, are you? Has something happened?'

How do I begin to answer that? I look at her hand that still holds mine, and think about running again. How far would we get? Before the world caught up with us.

'Yeah...' I say and swallow. 'My...'

And I'm shaking harder now, but I'm not cold, as Oona kneels and rubs my hand, my arm, and touches my face, where tears, that I didn't know were there, touch her fingers.

'Oh Sam, *shush* now. Oh Sam… *shush*, what is it, you can tell me, *shush* now…'

And I can, can't I? I can tell this girl from nowhere. Who I feel I could trust with everything, my life pushed into those warm, soft hands that stroke my face.

'My dad.'

I shake again, tears flooding my mouth. I'm like a toddler blubbing to his mum, all I need to do is cry and cry, until everything is all right, until she makes it better. She nods and goes, *shush, shush*, drawing it from me, this terrible thing I can't hold anymore.

'My dad's…'

A sound behind us. A cough. We both look round, and Chad is there, and he looks at me crying, at Oona close to me, at her holding my hands. He takes it in, and he knows.

'Sam, man…'

He comes forward and my tears turn cold, my belly hardens. I can't help it.

'Oh, Chad man, how great to see you!'

I stand and grin fiercely at him, wiping those flaming tears away.

'Sammy…'

'Had a good dance did you?'

Oona's looking at us both.

'Sam, come on…'

Chad's voice is calm and friendly. He reaches for me, but I flick his hand away.

'Sam, man, let's…'

'No, let's not, Chad man!'

I can't help it again. Chad's my best mate. He's done nothing wrong. A bit of dancing and flirting. That's what Chad does. That's why everyone likes him. That's why Oona likes him.

'Let's have a game of keepy-uppy instead, eh?'

I roll the manky football onto my foot, toe it and grab it out of the air. Chad watches me. Oona watches me.

'Sam, just calm…'

'Catch!'

I shove that ball, as if I'm shoving him, and Chad swerves and slips. The ball whams into the garage door, that shudders.

'Sam! What you doing?'

Chad's looking at me through that mop of hair, all tousled.

'I'm going home, Chad. What you doing?'

And I kick the ball so it whams again.

Then I turn from them both, from my mate who's good and charming, from the girl with the blackest eyes and the whitest teeth, the girl who cared, who held me.

I walk down the garden and out of the gate and run

into the street.

And keep running.

*

'*I'm tired, Dad, I can't walk anymore!*'

'*Ok, matey — how about a ride on the horse's back?*'

He bends down, dropping his knapsack.

'*Climb aboard, Captain.*'

I hold onto his shoulders and swing on, and Dad scoots my bum back, folding my legs under his arms.

'*Ready? Then we're off!*'

I giggle as he starts to canter through the grass.

'*Keep watching ahead, Sammy — we should see it soon!*'

I look over his shoulder as he neighs like a horse and tosses his mane.

'*Dad!*' *I laugh.*

'*What can you see?*' *He asks the question.*

'*A long hill, going up high.*' *I give the answer. Our little ritual. Just ours.*

'*Good, that means we're close!*'

We move on further, a few people clustering on the hillside, cagoules and walking boots. Dad said the White Horse has been a tourist spot for centuries, people coming to pay homage to that galloping, prancing figure on the hill.

We make the top, and the wind rushes up, makes me catch my breath. And it's strange, it's completely flat up here, a huge circle of land. A few people are standing on the bank, pointing and looking out.

'The Iron Age hill fort, Sam — this is where it would have been...'

I follow where he's pointing, imagining the wooden walls of the old fort. And as Dad talks, I see them, as though he's conjured them through time, villagers trotting to and fro. A goose pecking in the dirt. Guards keeping a watchful eye, until one of them hollers. An attack! A surge of an army climbing towards them...

'Come on, it's over here! Giddy up!'

Dadhorse neighs and canters across the green plain. A couple stop and stare.

'Dad! People think you're mad!'

'Who cares?' He gallops faster. 'Who cares when we've got the White Horse to see!'

We make the edge of the ridge and the world spills beneath us. Field upon field, and here and there, hills bump into a giant patchwork blanket that stretches across the land. Two birds hover against the clouds, strong wings defying the wind.

'Kites...' Dad checks himself. 'No. Ravens. Funny, you don't see them about here much.'

One screams, twisting and falling, then hovering steady. I know from Dad, that ravens aren't predators, but still I feel like its prey, feel its amber, killer eyes watching me, willing me to bolt.

'And here... Here we are at last...'

Dad points and I follow his finger. An edge of white chalk gouged into the turf.

'Where's the horse, Dad?'

He laughs, swings me higher onto his shoulders.

'Ah now, you see, that's the thing — the horse was made to be seen from far away, or from up high — I bet those birds have got the best view.'

I pull myself above Dad's head and peer down. I can make out a little more. A nose, an eye, the curve of a galloping leg. But I can't see it all. I look up at the watching ravens as they judder and shift in the wind.

'Why did they make it, Dad? If they couldn't see it...'

'Ah, but if you're over there...' Dad sets me down and sweeps his arm across the land. 'On those hills, or in those woods, then you'll see it, sure enough. A huge, great horse always running before your eyes.'

I imagine the people then, coming from miles and miles to stop and stare.

'Can we go there, so we can see it?'

'Surely, Sam...' He ruffles my hair as the ravens

call, and something makes me turn towards the hill. A tall, bearded man stands on the line of the hill, with two mighty dogs, brindled beasts. The wind catches his flowing hair.

'We'll go, for sure...'

'Dad — look at that man.'

Dad turns and looks. The man lifts his hand to the sky. And Dad waves.

'Do you know him, Dad?'

The man is walking, and now I can see that he's got a long walking stick, a staff in one hand.

'No. He's got big dogs, hasn't he? Alsatians, I think...'

The man lifts both his hands to the sky, and I realise that he isn't waving. He's summoning something. Something high above us.

'Dad! Look, the ravens!'

They spiral and screech through the air, coursing the wind, and as we watch, they plunge down, down towards the man's outstretched arms, two black gloves that fold about him.

'Well, I'll be...' Dad stares as the man stops and turns, the birds flapping close, the huge hounds at his side. 'Must be an animal trainer or something...'

Dad is quiet, as the man on the hill lifts his staff. And it's funny, it's as if he's calling to us now.

'Give him a wave then, Sam.' Dad kneels beside me. 'Maybe he'll bring us luck.'

Dad cups his hand and bellows.

'Hello! Hello!' And raises his arm to wave, and as I watch the man on the hill waves back.

'He is waving at us, Dad! He is waving!'

'Go on then, say hello!'

And I do, we both do, waving back to the animal man with his birds and dogs, until he stops and he turns and walks away below the brow of the ridge. Until we can only see his hair rising, lifting, a single raven hangs high then drops, and they are gone.

We're left, just me and Dad and the wind.